"You know you have to leave the bayou, Sabre," Kenyon said gently.

"I think of it," she replied.

"What do you think of, Sabre? Where?"

She stroked the oars through the mossy-green water, a contemplative smile on her pretty face, but then she shook her head, rowing on in silence. After a while she sighed deeply.

"Would my grandfather accept me, do you think?" she asked quietly.

He wanted to tell her what she wanted to hear, but he thought of Vanguard Garrick in that magnificent house in New Orleans, the hard, cold eyes, the rapacious smile. "I don't know, Sabre," he said at last, "but what have you got to lose by trying?"

She lifted the oars and let them hang a long moment before dipping them once more. "Only my pride," she told him. "Not a lot, perhaps—unless it's all you have."

Dear Reader;

This year marks our tenth anniversary and we're having a celebration! To symbolize the timelessness of love, as well as the modern gift of the tenth anniversary, we're presenting readers with a DIAMOND JUBILEE Silhouette Romance title each month, penned by one of your favorite Silhouette Romance authors.

Spend February—the month of lovers—in France with *The Ambassador's Daughter* by Brittany Young. This magical story is sure to capture your heart. Then, in March, visit the American West with Rita Rainville's *Never on Sundae*, a delightful tale sure to put a smile on your lips—and bring ice cream to mind!

Victoria Glenn, Annette Broadrick, Peggy Webb, Dixie Browning, Phyllis Halldorson—to name just a few—have written DIAMOND JUBILEE titles especially for you.

And that's not all! In March we have a very special surprise! Ten years ago, Diana Palmer published her very first romances. Now, some of them are available again in a three-book collection entitled DIANA PALMER DUETS. Each book will have two wonderful stories plus an introduction by the author. Don't miss them!

The DIAMOND JUBILEE celebration, plus special goodies like DIANA PALMER DUETS, is Silhouette Books' way of saying thanks to you, our readers. We've been together for ten years now, and with the support you've given to us, you can look forward to many more years of heartwarming, poignant love stories.

I hope you'll enjoy this book and all of the stories to come. Come home to romance—Silhouette Romance—for always!

Sincerely,

Tara Hughes Gavin
Senior Editor

ARLENE JAMES

A Perfect Gentleman

Silhouette Romance

Published by Silhouette Books New York

America's Publisher of Contemporary Romance

SILHOUETTE BOOKS
300 E. 42nd St., New York, N.Y. 10017

ISBN: 0-373-08705-5

First Silhouette Books printing February 1990

Printed in the U.S.A.

Books by Arlene James

Silhouette Romance

City Girl #141
No Easy Conquest #235
Two of a Kind #253
A Meeting of Hearts #327
An Obvious Virtue #384
Now or Never #404
Reason Enough #421
The Right Moves #446
Strange Bedfellows #471
The Private Garden #495
The Boy Next Door #518
Under a Desert Sky #559
A Delicate Balance #578
The Discerning Heart #614
Dream of a Lifetime #661
Finally Home #687
A Perfect Gentleman #705

ARLENE JAMES

grew up in Oklahoma and has lived all over the South. In 1976 she married "the most romantic man in the world." The author enjoys traveling with her husband, but writing has always been her chief pastime.

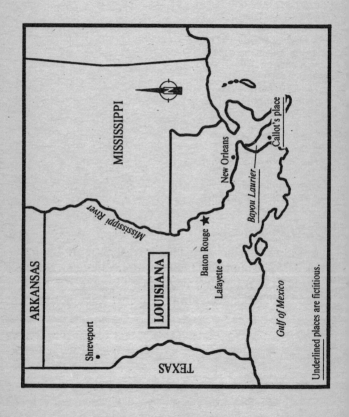

ARKANSAS

MISSISSIPPI

TEXAS

LOUISIANA

Mississippi River

Shreveport

Baton Rouge
Lafayette

New Orleans

Bayou Laurier

Callot's place

Gulf of Mexico

Underlined places are fictitious.

Chapter One

Kenyon pulled a crisp, white handkerchief from his hip pocket and mopped his forehead, shivering at the same time. He'd never been any place like the bayou. Or was it swamp? He had trouble telling the difference. It was hot and cold, all at once; with steamy fog rising off the murky, weed-clogged water and white shafts of sun piercing the dark overhead like crystalline pokers from some great furnace. The shiver was a product not only of the pervasive chill but also of the silence. It was eerie, oppressive and thick, even thicker than the air that made his lungs feel as if they were loosely stuffed with cotton. And he'd thought Houston was humid.

"How much farther?" he asked, addressing the back of the man who rowed in front of him. His own oar dripped dark stains onto the knees of his pleated khakis, but he'd stopped caring about such things within the first half hour of this unusual journey.

"A ways before we can start up the outboard." It came out, *"Ah waz b'fa we kin stat oop de oudbode."* The Cajun clip was so pronounced, in this case, that modern English sounded like a foreign language. Kenyon found it quite pleasant. He made a hobby of noting local accents and dialects and, in his opinion, Louisiana was replete with the most musical of them. He straightened and dipped his oar into the thick, green water.

"Can't be soon enough for me."

The man chuckled, the sinewy muscles beneath his faded chambray shirt flexing rhythmically. "I warned you. This here's a wild place. Ain't no street signs or numbered houses. Man, I known folks what lost their own way home after twenty year out here."

"I'm inspired with confidence in you, Piroux," Kenyon replied dryly.

"Just row the boat, man. Piroux will get you there. Yessir, the Callots better put the shrimps in the pot because we're a-comin.' "

Kenyon commented tersely that he couldn't wait for their arrival. Unlike New Orleans, which he found to be charmingly lazy, with a subtle European flavor and a blatant, thoroughly Dixie grace, the bayou made him think of dungeons and rats and shadowy mysteries better left undiscovered. It was, he reckoned wryly, very like the atmosphere of the Garrick household. Or was he simply projecting that unwelcome feeling upon his surroundings? He told himself not to be so cynical. The Callots might very well be different. There ought to be one mildly likable member of the family, one slightly deserving soul to receive the Garrick fortune when the old man finally descended into the abyss. Somehow, though, it didn't seem likely. *That Garrick gloom again,* he told himself and grimly slipped his oar into the water.

He concentrated on his stroke, pulling the oar smoothly back and up, blocking out everything but the physical effort required to keep the boat gliding swiftly through the clotted waters while Piroux steered it clear of debris and the tangling vegetation. Perspiration clung to Kenyon's skin like a clammy blanket, his clothing already limp and soggy-feeling from the humidity. They proceeded for some time in this manner, each man applying himself to his particular chore. They were friendly but not friends, alike in the way of all men, yet different in many ways, but with no objection on either's part to the pairing.

Gradually, the going became rougher. Gnarled cypress with spindly branches and mossy veils crowded together, surrounded by thorny, wiry thickets and banks of dirty debris. Twisted roots and sickly offshoots scraped the bottom of the canoe and grabbed at the blades of their oars as they passed. Eventually they were poling rather than paddling, the growth beneath the surface of the water making true paddling an impossibility. Some time later, Kenyon pulled up and slipped one hand into his jacket, waving at a buzzing insect with the other.

"Low-hanging branch," his guide advised quietly, and Kenyon bent double over his oar. Dappled light played on the bottom of the metal canoe, but the bright rays of sunshine no longer pierced the gloom in dazzling shafts, and a clammy chill was settling in, bringing the additional irritation of mosquitoes. A deep regret settled over Kenyon. The chain of decisions that had brought him here now seemed weak and corroded by poor judgment.

It was ironic. He'd been known to drive the length and breadth of the country, even to fly around the world with the news that someone had died. He'd traveled by auto, plane, bus, ship, train, bicycle, even horseback in Brazil. He'd visited farms and cities, embassies and flophouses, lumber camps and factories, hospitals, gold mines, artists' colonies, even a nunnery in Canada. He'd found heirs who'd wept at the news of their inheritances and others who had leaped and shouted for joy. Mostly, the reaction was stunned disbelief, and quite often there was swift disappointment when the size of the windfall was discovered. People too often imagined millions where thousands waited, and an unexpected piece of fortune became a disappointment grounded upon the specter of death. That wasn't so, in this case. In fact, this time the disappointment was his own.

Everyone involved should have been happy. The benefactor, though elderly and in ill health, was very much alive. That in itself was unique in his highly specialized law practice. There was the potential here of not only discovering family but of actually *reuniting* them, however distant. Yet, he'd known not one pleasant moment during the whole affair. In fact, the one potential heir he'd so far uncovered was the one person he could honestly say he disliked more than his client and his spinster sister. The Garricks were a truly disagreeable lot. Van was capricious and obstinate, and Mallory chilled a room with her mere presence, but it was the great-nephew, Darryl Garrick, who set his teeth on edge and sent a shiver down the back of his neck. He couldn't quite say why. It wasn't the man's oily manner, or his superior air that fueled Kenyon's dislike. It wasn't even his obvious greed. It was, rather, a vague sense of calamity accompanied by a sharp feeling of injustice. He kept asking himself why a truly impressive fortune should go to such an undeserving scoundrel, and he regretted being the agent through whom it had become possible.

So here he was, carefully working his way through the eerie closeness of the bayou, his muscles tired and aching, nerves on edge, a knot tightening in his stomach while he tracked another branch of the family that had so far caused him greater pangs of conscience and concern than any other he had encountered. What he wouldn't give to go back and do this over. He'd tell old man Garrick to look elsewhere for assistance, and then forget he'd even talked to him. If he'd only done that, he'd be sitting in a comfortable chair in a dry room sipping an excellent sherry, right now. The thought, so far from actuality, did not cheer him.

"We've found the canal," Piroux announced unceremoniously, and Kenyon perked up, suddenly attentive again. They were in a kind of clearing, a swath of space cut through the vegetation. The water felt deeper, colder, even darker, though he supposed that might be due to evening coming on. They lowered the small outboard motor, primed it and started it, exchanging places in the process. "Now we'll make time," Piroux said, "and a good thing. We best find someone to take us in, or we'll be spending the night on the water."

Kenyon lifted his arms, working a muscle in his back that objected to the hours of stroking. "I don't relish the idea of sleeping in this boat," he admitted, and the other man laughed.

"No one sleeps in an open boat in the bayou," he said. "He's too busy trying to keep from getting eaten alive." As if to make his meaning plain, a mosquito landed on Kenyon's bare forearm. The repellent he'd applied hours earlier seemed ineffective now. He swatted the bug and began digging in his duffel. When he uncapped the spray can, the Cajun chuckled and shook his head, but Kenyon ignored him. No secret code of the bayou, no macho attitude was going to cause him to make a meal of himself for a bunch of pesky insects. He was spraying again barely an hour later, and once true darkness descended, he understood. Mosquitoes didn't have to bite to make you miserable.

They traveled in darkness in order to make themselves less of a target, and gradually the swarms characteristic of the deep bayou abated somewhat. Then, in the distance, appeared a flickering pinprick of light.

"Sanctuary," the guide said, and Kenyon nodded. "If I'm not mistaken," the Cajun went on, "if this be the Bayou Laurier, for sure, that light could be our destination."

Hope surged in Kenyon. *Oh, let it be*, he said silently to whomever could hear, and he ran a hand through his straight, blond hair, smoothing it away from his forehead with a little flip. It was limp and heavy with moisture, but the gesture was merely automatic rather than the symptom of genuine concern for appearance. It gave him something to do as the tiny light grew slowly larger.

When he caught the first few notes, he thought they were some sort of natural phenomenon or his imagination. Then the seemingly disconnected notes became a clear strain, though strange and plunky and fast. He and the guide were within the feeble pool of light before he realized the odd, frenetic music came from a single instrument. *A banjo?* he wondered. *Or maybe a steel guitar?* Piroux cut the motor, and they glided closer. Kenyon saw a house, a small, weathered shack on stilts, wedged among the trees at the edge of the canal and fronted by a narrow wharf scarcely wider than the eaves of the sharp, plank roof. There were no windows that he could discern, but the door was a yellow rectangle of light. A small wood boat nearly bereft of flaking white paint bobbed on one corner of the wharf, where a small, rusty generator sat uncovered and silent. *No electricity*, he surmised correctly, and it came to him that he had taken a step backward in time.

"Hello, the house!" Piroux called, and the music abruptly ceased. A shadow appeared, and then a man moving slowly with what appeared to be a guitar in one hand. He was short and stocky, with a decided limp and an odd cant to his posture. Kenyon had the impression that he was an older man, but it was only an impression as the gloom hid his features.

Kenyon cupped his hands about his mouth. "Callot?" he shouted. "Lennox Callot?"

The man straightened, hitching backward, then slumped again. "Who wants to know?"

Piroux dipped an oar into the water, moving them swiftly forward. Kenyon waited until he could speak in a relatively normal tone of voice. "My name is Ames," he said, "Kenyon Ames, and I'm looking for the family of Gamelin Garrick Callot."

"Gamelin Callot is dead," the man said bluntly, and leaned both hands on the rail of the wharf. It creaked and gave enough so that Kenyon feared he'd pitch over into the dark water. He did not and didn't seem to fear that he would. Kenyon forced himself to relax, near enough now to see the man's face. It was as weathered as his house and bristled with a white, stubbly growth of beard.

"I realize Mrs. Callot is deceased," Kenyon said in as conversational a tone as he could manage. "It's her family in whom I'm interested. Might I come over, sir? I've news, important news."

Lennox Callot, for Kenyon was certain he had found him, growled in murky French and turned away. Kenyon looked at Piroux, who nodded toward the wharf at the very moment the prow of the boat bumped against it. Kenyon steeled himself and stood, swiftly but awkwardly. The little boat rocked beneath his feet. Piroux steadied it with a hand clasped to the rough pier, and Kenyon stepped up and forward. He turned back and stopped to hold the boat, but Piroux shook his head and indicated the door, through which Callot had disappeared. Kenyon pulled in a deep breath and followed, his smooth movements showing little of the hesitation he felt.

He stepped into the little room lit golden by the flames of a pair of mismatched hurricane lamps hanging from the canvas-covered ceiling. There were irregular, brown stains in several places, indicating that the roof above leaked badly. A narrow bunk had been built into one corner, its mattress and bedding rolled neatly at one end, and opposite it, also against the wall, stood a curtained cabinet. A propane camp stove sat atop it, and a variety of metal pans, pots and utensils hung from hooks hammered into the wall above. Beside was a small, square propane oven set upon cinder blocks. The only other furnishings were several narrow, backless benches that lined bare walls and a small, rectangular table in the center of the floor. Lennox Callot lowered himself stiffly into the one chair at that table, his guitar propped against it. He looked at Kenyon blandly.

"Well, don't hang in the door."

Kenyon walked swiftly forward. Callot waved him down onto a bench. He sat and leaned forward, elbows on knees, hands clasped before him. It was only then that he noticed her, a girl standing silently in the darkened doorway of another room near the kitchen area. At first, he saw only slender, bare legs beneath the hem of a full, flowered skirt. It was enough to lift his gaze upward in interest, following the gently flaring curves of rounded thighs and hips and the small, nipped-in waist above which were folded smooth, graceful arms and tiny hands. She moved, then, crossing one bare foot in front of the other, and leaned against the door post. His eyes lifted automatically to her face, past full, voluptuous breasts and a slender, creamy neck bare of the tight, flowered bodice.

Simply put, she was lovely. Her heart-shaped face was framed by dark, thick hair that curled languidly about her shoulders and temples. Her brows were wispy wings on her pale face, her mouth full and lush, her nose petite and delicate, her eyes round and wide and rimmed with dark lashes. Her chin was a pert, little thing and slightly pointed, her cheeks round and dimpled. She gave her head a toss, as if to say she was used to being looked at, and her eyes, when his met them, were bright and bold and guardedly curious.

"Sabre," the older man said, identifying her as his daughter, "we'll have a drink from that jar cooling in the bayou."

Kenyon started to decline, but then she stepped forward and crossed the room, her slender arms swinging gracefully at her sides, and he found his voice had suddenly disappeared. He swallowed and smiled lamely, switching his gaze to her father as she passed through the door, her short skirt flipping out behind her. After breathing deeply, he began his explanation, noting the scowl with which Lennox Callot greeted the name of Vanguard Garrick. The girl came back with a gallon jar filled to the lid with brown liquid and tied with a wet rope. The front of her dress was wet, and she left a spattered, snaky trail behind her, but Callot didn't pay the least heed. Kenyon went on as best he could, clearing his throat, for it had suddenly become scratchy.

"Um, it's my business, you see. I'm an attorney, and I specialize in estate planning and inheritance cases. That's why Mr. Garrick hired me. He wants to—how shall I say?— put his house in order, finalize his will. In other words, he's ready to choose an heir and—"

"Vanguard Garrick is a mean, nasty, greedy, old son-of—"

"Maybe *Grand-père* has changed." The girl interrupted her father less forcefully than he'd interrupted Kenyon, but the effect was far superior. Her silky voice, embroidered with a languid accent, seemed to stroke the air, soothing Lennox Callot into reluctant silence. She set a small jar of the brown liquid in front of him on the table and carried another to Kenyon, her movements slow and swaying and graceful. Kenyon took the jar from her, his attention alternating between its contents and its bearer. She smiled lazily, looking down at him from beneath the lids of exotic, golden eyes. "It is tea, brewed by the sun and cooled by the bayou," she told him. He nodded a thank-you and sipped the amber liquid, savoring the rich, smooth flavor. The bayou was not without its small pleasures, after all.

"Perhaps," she said, sauntering back to her father's side, "my grandfather has found a way to overcome his pride and reunite his family, no, *Monsieur*...?" She cocked an eyebrow in his direction, the lamplight making a dark fire of her hair.

"Ames," Kenyon supplied. "Kenyon Ames."

"*Monsieur* Ames," she said, and laid a hand upon her father's shoulder. He shook his head, scowling, but remained quiet. "You must forgive my father. He is not a well man, and the memories of an old, sick man are deep and sharp. My mother, you see, was a very beautiful woman, and wealthy and educated—a rare woman. To have a woman like that, to be chosen by her, to see her happy in a place like this, a place so far from what she might have had, and then to see her do without, to grow old too soon, to die too early, such a thing can make a man bitter."

Kenyon shook himself loose of the musical effect of her voice and prepared a careful reply. "I understand that Garrick disinherited her."

"And cursed her, as well," she said. "He killed her the day she chose my father. He killed her memory from his heart. She had no father from that day."

"It was Mardi Gras," the old man said wistfully. "She was dressed as a queen, and I fell at her feet. I begged her to marry me, on the spot." He shrugged. "A man will do strange things at times, things he would not do in any other moment. I still remember the look in her eyes, fear at first, then a smile." He shook his head mournfully. "Such a smile!"

Kenyon found himself measuring the awe a man like this would feel for a well-bred woman. Had she regretted her decision? he wondered, and looked about him quickly. *Almost without doubt,* he told himself. How could she not? Probably the old man knew it, but he couldn't bring himself to give her up. Still, she needn't have stayed. Unless . . . Of course. Where could she go after being disinherited? He was aware of the murmur of voices and the fluid whisper of movement. He looked up to see Sabre standing before him, a framed photograph in her delicate hands.

"Show him!" the old man said with a raspy voice, tears clouding his eyes. Sabre thrust the photo forward, and Kenyon trained his eyes upon it, surprised to see a rather average-looking, middle-aged woman, a bit plump, with her dark hair plaited in a braid at the nape of her neck. Her skin was rather pallid, her eyes too pale, but the smile was genuine and wide. He detected the familial resemblance between this woman and Mallory Garrick, but there was none of the coldness and bitterness of the latter. Could Gamelin Callot have been happy? Perhaps being adored was enough for some women, but a Garrick? He had a hard time believing in the kind of love that could overcome such differences in background and breeding. He lifted his gaze to Sabre's. Lust could be a powerful emotion for a man, he mused, and for some women. Was Gamelin Garrick Callot such a woman? Was her daughter?

The old man was weeping and wiping his eyes with gnarled, hoary hands. Kenyon switched his attention elsewhere. Lennox Callot had loved his wife, he decided. That was understandable. She had been the unattainable, suddenly, magically attained. But could that, alone, have sustained them here in this place? It was a mystery to him, he conceded privately, and no longer of any import. It was time to direct the conversation back to the matter at hand.

"It seems to me," he began carefully, "that your family is entitled to a share of the Garrick estate. Obviously, Vanguard Garrick is willing to consider such a possibility or I wouldn't be here. He would like to meet his grandchildren, to get to know them. I'm sure their mother would approve considering—"

"Their mother would as soon have given them a full-grown 'gator for a pet," the old man boomed, but a gentle squeeze of his daughter's hand upon his shoulder calmed him instantly. "I tell you," he growled up at her, "the Garricks're poison, all of 'em—'cept your mother, God rest her soul."

"It's getting late, Papá," she told him quietly. "You are tired, and our guests will want a bed."

The old man scowled nastily, but the weight of his daughter's hand upon his shoulder seemed considerable. At last, he nodded. "You and your man will need a bed for the night," he said. The girl patted his shoulder approvingly and moved toward the shelf in the corner.

"Will you have a taste of rum in your tea, Mr. Ames?" she asked, reaching for a small, brown, unlabeled bottle.

"Ah, no, thank you. The tea is delicious. My guide, however..."

"Of course."

She carried the bottle to the table, unstoppered it, and poured a dram into the old man's jar. The rum swirled greasily in the amber liquid. The old man hunched over it, sightless, sad, lost in his memories. Sabre set the bottle on the table and replaced the rubber cork. Her eyes found Kenyon's and held them placidly.

"*Monsieur* Piroux," she called, and the guide immediately appeared in the doorway, with Kenyon's duffel and his own smaller one slung over his shoulder. The man said something in garbled French, and she replied in kind. He nodded and walked across the floor, disappearing through the other door. "You must share the room," she told Kenyon lightly, "but there are two beds with a curtain between them for privacy. This way, eh?" She turned and sauntered toward the door through which the guide had passed, pausing to look over her shapely shoulder. "If you please, *monsieur*."

Kenyon swallowed a gulp of his tea and stood, realizing he was staring. He carried the jar to the table and left it, wondering whether to speak to the old man or not. He looked to the girl and received the barest shake of her pretty head. Thus warned, he followed silently.

The glow of light extended only inches into the darkened room, but Sabre moved quickly and surely through the darkness. Kenyon waited, his eyes slowly adjusting, and caught the breathtaking silhouette of a girl, very much a woman, against the gray square of a window. Then a match flared in her hand and she lit a candle on a small, rough table. A soft illumination filled the room, revealing Piroux rolled in a blanket upon one of the narrow beds, his face to the wall, boots placed neatly beside him on the floor. The other bed was covered with a faded floral spread and a small, round, lace pillow. Undoubtedly it was the girl's, Sabre's, bed.

"It's all right," she said, as if reading his thoughts. "There is a bed in the rafters." She indicated a simple ladder nailed to the wall beside the door, and Kenyon's gaze followed it upward to where the ceiling should have been. He could see glimmers of starlight through the cracks of the roof.

"I don't want to put you out of your bed," he began awkwardly, but she merely laughed, the sound deep and throaty.

"Would you prefer to climb the ladder?" she asked teasingly. "Or aren't you afraid you might put your foot wrong and fall through the canvas onto my father's head?"

He smiled. "On second thought, thank you for sharing your bed, ah, giving up. I meant to say, giving up your bed." He fought the impulse to bite his tongue, and darted a glance at Piroux. The man seemed dead, so still was he. *Well, what of it?* Kenyon thought defensively. *Men are men, aren't they? A gentleman will keep his hands to himself, of course.* He put his behind him and forced himself to look around the small room calmly.

To his surprise, there were books everywhere—under the beds, in boxes at the foot of each, stacked beneath the little table and lined up along the window sash and on shelves on the narrow wall opposite them. Most of them were paperbacks, though there were some old and musty hardbacks in one corner. He took the candle from the table and carried it to the shelves, quickly scanning the titles.

"Perhaps you would like to borrow one," she suggested smoothly. "I could recommend something."

He gave her a sharp glance and continued his perusal. "Well, I am impressed. I didn't know you could get Bunyan and Congreve in paperback, let alone the Rosettis. Dante is my favorite."

"And Christina, mine," she came back confidently.
"Now I am impressed. I didn't expect a lawyer to be quite so well-read."

"I toyed with the idea of being an English professor before I settled on the law."

A wistful smile crossed her face. "I would study literature," she stated firmly, then lightened her tone. "I am a seller of books," she said, waving her hand at the boxes. "These—" she crossed to the wall of shelves and ran her fingers lightly over the tattered spines "—these I cannot bear to part with, not that there is much of a market for the classics here in the bayou. Still, I make a bit of money with the others. My brother picks them up in secondhand stores and such, and I sell them, very cheaply, to our neighbors— some of them, anyway." She smiled gamely and lifted her chin, shoulders erect. The effect was a pronounced thrust of her ample breasts. Kenyon felt his mouth go dry.

"Well," he said, turning away, "that displays a commendable ambition, as well as an imaginative approach to creating business." He moved his duffel from the bed to the floor, then found himself at a loss. What should he do? Start undressing for bed? He looked at Piroux, fully clothed beneath his blanket, and put the idea firmly out of mind.

"Did you like school?" she asked suddenly, and he turned with a surprised look.

"I beg your pardon?"

"College," she said, her face more animated than any time before. "My brother—"

"That would be Butler," he put in, and she nodded.

"He is nineteen, very bright, so much promise. He should really go to college, you understand? It's our dream, the two of us, college."

Kenyon blinked at her, not sure he understood. "Your brother would like to attend college," he said, feeling stupid.

"Both of us!" she declared. "But it is Butler who should really go. I hate to think of him working seven-day weeks on that shrimp boat with only a visit home, now and then. Papá hates it, too. It is bad for a man used to hard work to sit at home nursing his pains while his children labor to support him."

"It's his back, isn't it?" Kenyon asked, having observed the man's difficulty with moving.

She bit her lip and nodded. "It hurts him constantly, every moment, but he never complains. He is too proud." She looked down at her hands, now fumbling at fingertips. "Perhaps you did not know that a poor man can be proud." Abruptly, she lifted her chin, pinning him with her golden eyes. For a moment his breathing seized. He swallowed a lump in his throat that was caused by nothing whatever to do with the subject being discussed.

"You know, you've just given me two excellent reasons why you ought to take your grandfather up on his proposal," he said carefully. "There are no guarantees, of course, but it could work out in your favor."

"And it could not," she returned quickly.

"True, but isn't it worth the effort?"

She folded her arms beneath her full breasts. "I am not so sure. We have good reason to distrust Vanguard Garrick. I know, for a fact, that my mother feared him. He was very cruel to her. I would like to think that he has realized his mistake and longs to know his grandchildren, to reunite his family, but..." She shook her head, the dark tresses flashing red in the candlelight.

He took a different tack. "Sabre, do you know what kind of money we're talking about here?" he asked, purposefully omitting any talk of family. "I wonder if you understand what's at stake." Quietly, he named a figure that assessed the current minimum Garrick holdings, the ones of which he knew, anyway.

Sabre's mouth dropped open, and a look of pure horror widened her eyes. "You're making that up!"

He wanted to laugh; instead, he shook his head solemnly. "Not at all. It's a great deal of money, enough to let pass a lot of unpleasantness."

Her eyes narrowed sharply. "I don't think I like what you are suggesting."

"All I'm suggesting is that you ought not to pass up this opportunity to help your family."

"I think what you are suggesting is a sin," she retorted.

He laughed nervously and shook his head again. "No, Sabre, really, I'm just thinking of your family. Shouldn't family inherit, after all? Certainly you have as much right as your cousin."

She bit her lip again. It was rather a pouty lip, full and red. Kenyon scratched his nose, diverting his own attention. She was altogether too attractive a girl. *Woman*, he automatically amended, his gaze going right back where he didn't want it to go.

"If only he really wanted family around him," she said tremulously. "It would be so easy to go to him with love and forgiveness, then."

"I think that's rather unrealistic," he countered. "I do know something of the history here, and looking at it objectively, I think a justifiable case can be made on either side. He lost a daughter; she lost a father. Who can say who should beg forgiveness of whom?"

Suddenly, those leonine eyes were sparking angrily. "And do you agree, then, with what he did to her? He killed her. He made her dead to him. Because she loved my father, he took his own love away."

"I never said your family owed him anything. I understand the enmity."

"And does that justify going after his fortune?" she demanded. "Should we exact recompense in dollars?"

"I didn't say that. I only said it's a lot of money, money your family seems to need. Besides, it can't hurt to try. You have as much right to the Garrick family fortune as any other family member. What can you lose by letting your grandfather get to know you? All right, he's a stodgy, autocratic old snob. He said nothing about mending family rifts. If you want to know the truth, I have my doubts he'll share so much as a nickel with you and your brother, either before or after his death. But how will you ever know what the possibilities are, if you don't try? All he asks is that one, or both, of you comes to New Orleans. Let him get to know you, make your case."

"And then what? Come home and wait for him to die?" she shot back.

He shook his head in exasperation. "Believe me, whoever Garrick chooses will earn the inheritance. The heir is expected to remain in New Orleans with him."

She screwed up her pretty face. "And the other is banished! It sounds a cruel game to me."

"Perhaps it is," he conceded, "but is it any more cruel than seven-day weeks on a shrimper, or the silent suffering of someone you love?"

She sent him a pointed look, then quickly dropped her gaze. "Perhaps Butler should go," she muttered, but they both knew Butler couldn't afford to give up that seven-days-a-week job. That job fed them, clothed them, bought the rum and aspirin that made her father's pain bearable. Her pretty mouth turned down in a pouty frown. "I need time to think," she said, pushing her hands into her auburn hair. "Will you give me time to think?"

"Sure," he told her quietly, sensing her ambivalence and desperation. "Take a day or so and mull it over." He looked at the still form of Piroux upon the shabby bed. "Of course, we'll, um, pay for room and board."

Her mouth turned upward again in a cynical smile. "This is the bayou, *monsieur*. Guests do not pay for hospitality."

"You didn't invite us here," he stated firmly. "Besides, it goes on the expense account. Let Garrick pay."

She put her hands to her hips and laughed, tilting her pretty head back. "Yes, *monsieur*, let Garrick pay. I am not so proud as that!"

She bade him good-night, then, and mounted the ladder. He looked away as she went over the top into the dark attic, her skirt gathered in one hand. He sat down on her bed and began to remove his shoes, speaking to the darkness overhead.

"By the way, my name is Kenyon, remember? Why don't you use it? *Monsieur* is a bit formal, don't you think?"

For a moment, there was nothing but silence. He blew out the light and lay down. The bed was surprisingly comfortable, not too soft, not too hard, no lumps. He imagined her here in his place, and the image brought feelings with which he was not prepared to deal. He turned them off immediately, lifting his arm across his eyes as if to physically block them out. Then her laughter wafted down to him, as soft as the lapping of the water against the pier.

"Kenyon Ames," she said. "It's a good name for a lawyer. Good night, Kenyon."

"Good night, Sabre." *Sabre*, he thought, *a good name for a delectable little vixen.* He scolded himself and rolled over onto his side, sleep drawing near already, but he couldn't stop one more thought. Would he be throwing her to the hounds if he left her with Van Garrick?

Chapter Two

Kenyon leaned forward and braced his elbows on the railing, enjoying the fresh, clean feel of morning on his face and the cup of warm chicory-laden coffee in his hands. A fly buzzed nearby, but he ignored it, too content to be troubled by such small irritations. He had slept much more soundly than he'd expected, so much so that he hadn't even heard the girl come down from her perch among the rafters or the stirring of her father in the other room. When Kenyon had awakened, he'd seen Piroux sitting up in his narrow bed, yawning, his head in his hands. Sabre had been singing in a soft, sweet voice as she prepared breakfast. A feeling of deep well-being had come to him, and it lingered still, through a Spartan meal and a cold-water shave and a third cup of coffee. He smiled into the cup. He never drank three cups of coffee in a single morning, and he didn't like chicory.

Sabre stepped outside and smiled at him as she walked to the end of the little porch. A small winch was fastened to the side of the house there, like an oversized reel from a fishing pole. Sabre knelt and cranked the little handle, drawing in a small, thick chain and the shabby boat attached to it. When the boat clumped against the side of the house, she reached out, pulled it around and moored it, bow and stern, to the narrow pier. Kenyon watched, savoring the moment and the sunlight dancing on the dark water. Humming, she rose and strolled past him, tugging at the hem of her soft T-shirt where it rode up past the waistband of her jeans. They weren't much, as jeans went. Cropped just below the knees and faded to a pale blue, they had white, scraggly fringes and clung to her gently rounded shape like a second skin. She wore rubber thongs on her feet, and they squished and flopped as she strode by; yet, somehow, she managed to be graceful and sensuous. Kenyon shook his head as she disappeared into the house.

Only seconds passed before she reappeared, a net bag of books in both hands. She was biting her lip in deep thought, but she spared him another quick smile and a shake of her head when he offered to help. She hefted the bag into the boat and brushed her hands together before following them, stepping down smoothly onto the ribbed bottom. She settled herself on the rowing seat in the center of the boat, forced the oars into the locks, and grasped a haft in each hand.

"Want to come along?" she asked, staring up at him. "For certain, you have nothing better to do."

She didn't have to ask twice. He wondered where they were going, but it didn't really matter. He tossed his coffee dregs into the water and ducked inside to leave the cup on the table. She kept her seat while he gingerly let himself down into the little boat.

He supposed the gentlemanly thing to do was to volunteer for the roughest duty.

"I'll row," he said, but she shook her head.

"No, I'll do it."

"No, really, I want to."

"But you don't know where we're going!"

"You can show me!"

"I was here first, Ames!"

They looked at each other and laughed at their childishness.

"You row," he said, facing her as he sat in the bottom of the boat.

She cast off one line, and he cast off the other. Then she pushed away from the pier and dipped her oars into the water, pulling a long, smooth stroke that slid them backward as if on oiled glass. Easily, one oar steering, the other propelling, she turned them south and began the slow, measured pace that moved them downstream. Kenyon scratched an ear, knowing he was clearly outclassed. She smiled at him, her strong, young arms drawing and releasing the oars. He thought, as he watched her, that more young women ought to take up rowing, and then he realized he was staring and turned his head, pretending to watch the foliage that slid by.

Soon they turned off into a narrow inlet overhung with low boughs shrouded in moss. The air was very still here and overlaid with the trills and clicks of birds and insects. Suddenly they came upon a shanty wedged between two trees at bank's edge. The house was not properly settled on piers sunk deeply into the soft, wet earth. It leaned to one side and slightly forward, making its stoop, perhaps a foot square, impossible to stand upon. A very old man came to the open door and peered out, shading misted eyes with trembling, gnarled hands. When he recognized Sabre, a smile of greeting cracked his face, showing a conspicuous lack of teeth.

"Montegut," she called him, and their chatter was lively and puzzling. The clipped, slurred, elongated syllables were spoken too rapidly for Kenyon to follow, and the exchange was sprinkled with unfamiliar French Cajun phrases. The old man seemed lonely, and Sabre obligingly entertained him with bright synopses of the books in her bag.

The old man leaned from his doorway, taking each offering in his rough, cracked hands. He drew back after a moment and appeared again, wearing thick, enormous glasses that made his eyes look like doves' eggs with flat, gray yolks. Carefully, he thumbed and read and turned over each book as if it were a precious object. Finally, he made his selection, and a price was negotiated, after which he offered as trade-in a slender, hardback volume entitled, *A Guide to Wet Farming*. After proper consideration, Sabre valued it at ten cents and received forty more in coin, which the old man took, penny by penny, from a zippered change purse fetched from some hiding place within the shack.

After a few more minutes of conversation, Sabre took her leave at last. They turned back the way they had come, returning to the Bayou Laurier, then heading south. Once more they were moving through dense growth, much of it broken and twisted. This trip was fruitless, however. They stopped at three places, each an amalgamation of tin and lumber. At one house, children peered from a doorway, watching with fingers in mouths as their mother hung clean laundry on a line strung between the corner of her small home and a tree. Sabre left them a small storybook, though their mother declined to buy it.

Back to the Laurier they went, ducking low to avoid the overhanging branches, and on southward until they came to another inlet, this one better defined than the others. They spent some time moving along this narrow canal. There were fine homes here, fine by backwater standards, neat, sound houses with strong pilings and clean, sturdy piers. The land was more compact here and slightly higher than elsewhere along the bayou, allowing room for small vegetable gardens and utility buildings. Mostly, there was no one home, but on occasion they found a housewife willing to purchase a book or two. Most of them knew Sabre well, and she was obviously at ease with them, but the trip took considerable time, as it was necessary to leave the boat and walk up the piers to knock on closed doors. After the second stop, Kenyon put himself in the rowing seat and glared at her as she climbed aboard, lest she object. But she merely smiled at him and lowered herself, cross-legged, to the bottom of the boat, the corner of a dollar bill peeking out from her jeans' pocket.

He began to row, rather awkwardly at first, but then more smoothly, expecting the short distances between stops to be a boon. Wrong. Getting going was by far the most difficult portion of the task; no sooner would he hit a comfortable stride, than it would be time to pull up again. Kenyon considered himself in pretty good shape. He worked out regularly, played tennis with a dedication just short of obsession, and made a point of lifting weights two or three times a week, but that didn't stop the pain from building at the tops of his shoulders and the center of his back and chest, not to mention his knees. He shifted his position slightly, relieving the strain on his legs or, rather, properly redistributing it. Gradually he found the best technique for double-oar rowing. The silent looks Sabre sent his way told him that she noticed and approved, but he wasn't foolish enough to think he was going to get away scot-free with this little experiment. He was going to pay with soreness and fatigue. Still, like a schoolboy, he took a certain amount of pride in those quiet, frank looks.

It was much smoother going out in the canal proper. Their final stop was, like the Callot place, right on the marshy bank. This site looked new. Soil had been dredged and diked with fat, oiled poles sunk deeply beneath the water. The pilings were set in concrete, the wharf, unweathered, the nails, shiny and silver and tight. The house was a small trailer, little more than a storage shed, but new and clean and neat, with a satellite dish for television reception mounted just behind it. Someone had attached flower boxes to the windows, and a few scraggly daisies were already poking up through the dark earth. A cheap lawn chair made of aluminum tubes and nylon webbing sat beside the front door. As Kenyon and Sabre drew near the dock, an obviously pregnant young woman came out and lowered herself into it.

"Hello, Mrs. Caradyne," Sabre called. The young woman's face lit with a smile. "How are you doing today?" Sabre kept up a steady stream of polite questions to which the woman replied shyly and softly while Kenyon concentrated on docking the boat. "This is Mr. Ames," Sabre said before climbing up onto the pier. "He's helping me today. Would you like to see what I've got?"

The woman, a girl really, nodded silently, and Sabre reached down for the net bag full of her wares. Quickly, Kenyon seized the bag and swung it up to her, and for a moment their eyes caught and held. Hers were a very light brown with spokes of yellow that gave them the glint of gold. They were shaded by thick, rust-colored lashes. He thought, in that moment, that he'd never seen anything quite so beautiful. Then suddenly the lids were coming down over those bright orbs, and a kind of self-consciousness came over him, so that he looked away before the lids lifted again and those yellow spokes impaled him. It was a moment only, almost unnoticeable in the flow of movements, and yet it left him flushed with a strange sort of heat.

Sabre took the bag and stood smoothly, turned, and strode lightly along the pier. The two women talked at first of the weather and the problem of mice and other small creatures that tended to take up residence in one's house. Sabre suggested that a sprinkling of crushed sage around windowsills and cabinet doors kept ants out of the kitchen, while a cat was the only sensible solution for mice, unless one preferred snakes. When the woman wondered where she could get one, Sabre promised to keep an eye out for a weaning litter.

Soon, they got down to the subject of books. It was so lonely, the young wife said, and she liked to read, but some stories frightened her, and with her man gone so much, it was best not to add anxiety. Might Sabre have something useful, a volume on child care, perhaps? Like a genie dipping into her bottle, Sabre produced the very item, and a work on pregnancy and childbirth, too. Before she was done, the woman had decided on not only both "practical" volumes but a mystery and a historical saga, as well. Sabre came back to the dinghy with her bag almost empty and her pockets almost full.

The day had brought her twelve dollars and some change, which she delightedly counted as they glided back the way they had come. Kenyon couldn't help being amused with her particular brand of commerce.

"You must think I'm pitiful," she said, her bubbly tone belying any real concern.

"Well...you're enterprising...I'll give you that much," he managed between strokes.

"And from you, I think perhaps that is a lot."

He only grinned and continued to row, but he was tired and the muscles in his upper arms weren't about to let him pretend otherwise. They quivered and rippled beneath the skin.

"You should let me take the oars, now," she said mildly. Going up on her knees, she pressed her hands against his forearms. "I insist."

He protested just enough to satisfy his masculine pride, before pulling the oars in and propping them. She sat back on her heels and pushed tendrils of dark red-brown hair out of her face, smiling at him with the most naked, blatant appreciation he'd ever seen on a woman's face. The effect was positively erotic, not just inviting but compelling. He couldn't have stayed away from her if he'd wanted to—and he didn't.

He slid off the seat onto his knees, and as he reached for her, the expression on her face changed to one of languid expectation. She came to him slowly, deliberately, rising up off her heels, dark hair trailing behind her, slender arms gliding around his neck. Long, dark lashes drooped over golden eyes and fluttered to rest against pale olive skin as their lips met, tentatively at first and then with growing force. His arms closed about her, bringing firm, feminine curves to yield against him. She was magnificent, this dainty, voluptuous swamp kitten, made for a man's arms, all woman and all heat—and all wrong. He pictured himself making love to her right there in the dinghy, or behind the curtain on her little bed back at the shanty. But try as he might, he couldn't see himself walking into the *Chez Louis* with Sabre Callot on his arm. He couldn't see her sitting to dine at his mother's table or running the ball down on the court at the club. He felt like a heel, and the longer he plied that delicious kiss, the more of a heel he felt. And yet it was she who found a stopping place, who broke their mouths apart and sank back onto the bottom of the boat.

"Well," she said with a lazy purr, "now we know, hmm?"

Kenyon lifted a hand to her cheek, despite himself. "You're a lovely woman, Sabre." He had to tell her; he couldn't keep it to himself. Her laugh was deep and throaty.

"And you are a lovely man, but I cannot stay and play. You make me forget too easily that soon you will be gone." She stretched and got herself up, moving easily past him to take up the oars. "Tell me, Kenyon Ames," she said, "where will you soon be gone to?"

He told her about Houston—about the big, empty house he kept there and the bigger, emptier one where his mother lived alone, now that her husband was deceased and her sons were on their own. He talked about nieces and nephews and a pair of sisters-in-law who had little use for a single brother who could come and go as he pleased and did so with regularity. He told her about the office he kept in the penthouse of the high-rise building his father had built with the money that had flowed in from the oil wells he'd punched in the ground. He talked about cases that had taken him to far, dusty places and about little, old ladies who had lived lonely and Spartan lives and left fortunes to be claimed by relatives never seen or known. He told her more than he had intended.

"Such interesting work," she said, "must keep a man from thinking of settling down. My father would say a job makes a poor wife, but he never wanted to leave this place, never needed to see beyond it. I suppose every man has his own satisfaction. Every woman, too."

"And what's your satisfaction, Sabre? Selling used books from door to door?"

She smiled thinly. "There is satisfaction in surviving, is there not?" she said, pulling smoothly on the oars. "I am satisfied to survive, Ames. Anyway, I try to be."

He pulled his knees up and rested his forearms atop them. "You know you have to leave here, Sabre," he said gently.

"I think of it."

"What do you think of, Sabre? Where?"

She stroked the oars through the mossy green water, a contemplative smile on her pretty face, but then she shook her head, rowing on in silence. After a while she pulled a deep breath.

"Would he accept me, do you think?" she asked quietly.

He wanted to tell her what she wanted to hear, but he thought of Vanguard Garrick in that magnificent house in

New Orleans, the hard, cold eyes, the rapacious smile. "I don't know, Sabre," he said, at last, "but what have you got to lose by trying?"

She lifted the oars and let them hang a long moment before dipping them once more. "Only my pride," she told him. "Not a lot, perhaps, unless it's all you have."

She shrugged and concentrated on her rowing, silently reminding him that she usually did this alone. He could not help thinking of the measure of desperation that provoked so much activity for so little return. He looked at her, smiling and rowing and smiling and rowing, and he thought of Darryl Garrick, with his soft hands and his oily leer. Kenyon's stomach twisted into hard knots. It seemed so unfair that a shyster like Darryl could hold the inside track on inheriting a fortune the size of the Garrick family's while a sweet, hardworking young woman such as Sabre—who really needed a break, by the way—remained on the outside. On the other hand, would simple, honest, unsophisticated Sabre be decent competition for worldly-wise Darryl? Inside, Kenyon had his doubts, serious doubts. After all, when everything was said and done, Sabre Callot remained a backwater bumpkin, while Darryl, as distasteful as he was, had been raised in an upper-class atmosphere. Darryl fitted the mold. Sabre did not. Still, Vanguard Garrick was nothing if not mercurial. There was a possibility...

He tried to put the matter out of mind. He'd taken too much initiative as it was, and of more than one kind. He'd done his job already, and shortly he'd be leaving the Garricks and Callots to their own solutions. In fact, as soon as it was decent and practical to do so, he'd be on his way. Suddenly he regretted the promise to give her time, the involvement, however minor, in her seemingly bleak existence. Something told him Sabre Callot could suck a man right out of his world and into hers if he wasn't careful. He would keep his distance, he told himself, but then he caught that innocent smile, that sweet-as-candy, bright-as-light, seductive smile, and he felt his own mouth turn up in tender, automatic response. Whatever else she was, this woman was not powerless. Oh, no. Not at all. But then again, he was no anxious, virginal adolescent, eager to fall beneath the spell of any female's charm, however potent. He felt better for having reminded himself of that fact, and a little foolish.

He looked away, and something caught at his ear, a faint, lilting distraction. Then suddenly there was music! He didn't know if, in his preoccupation, he'd missed the first distinct notes or if this reeling tune had simply burst forth in high, full-bodied tone. It seemed that one moment the bayou slid by them in eerie silence and the next it was filled with a strange, wordless song. Sabre froze, the wild music seeming to swirl about her, then erupted with movement. The dinghy shot forward, the water churning with her pull and release of the oars. She was smiling, then laughing, her strong young arms working like jackhammers. Within moments they hove into view of the Callot shanty, but it wasn't the tiny house that they saw. Kenyon turned on his knee in the little dinghy, his mouth slightly ajar as he took in the large, high-prowed boat filling the bayou with its spire-like antennae and winches spiking through the overhanging foliage.

Sabre whooped and waved an arm over her head, calling, "Jeanetta! Hoo, Jeanetta!" Kenyon strained to see whom she greeted, and caught the top of a dark head. From the height of it, he judged the head to belong to a child, and from the name, he surmised the child to be a girl. Oddly, the child didn't return the greeting. Instead, the dark head disappeared from view altogether. Within seconds, Sabre had maneuvered them around the stern of the boat. It was hard to tell what was moored to what, the boat to the shanty or the shanty to the boat. Again, Sabre called out to the girl, who leaned against the wharf railing. The sound of Sabre's voice was all but drowned out by the crazy music coming from the house. The child turned her back to them.

"She didn't hear you," Kenyon observed loudly.

"She heard me," was the flat reply. "That's Jeanetta Goula, daughter of friend Ami, and that's his shrimper."

His? Kenyon could only stare at the big boat. Yes, of course, he'd seen shrimp boats before, but at a distance. As for the child and the friend, well, he'd never seen a more sullen girl or known a man named Ami. He helped Sabre tie up at the end of the narrow wharf, and offered her a hand up, but she was already on her way, unaware and unneedful of his offered assistance. She practically leaped from the boat, her excitement matching the frenetic intensity of the music. She paused on her way to the door to slip an arm about the girl, a scruffy-looking child wearing jeans ripped at the hems and dirty sneakers. There were holes at the knees and stains on the seat; the pocket had been almost torn off her dark plaid shirt and left to hang limply by one tattered corner. Her thick hair was a mass of tangles that had been cropped at the nape of her neck and left without the attention of a comb. She shrugged out of Sabre's hug and turned once more to stare at the water, leaving Sabre to hurry on her way.

Kenyon hauled himself up out of the little boat, bringing Sabre's net bag with him. The child turned to stare at him with oddly blank eyes, but turned away the instant he spoke.

"Hello," he said, then cleared his throat and moved along, curious about the girl and the friend and the boat and the music that suddenly stopped.

Kenyon turned toward the door and stepped forward. There stood Sabre on tiptoe in the center of the small room, her arms wrapped tightly about the neck of a fairly tall young man with shaggy brown hair. He had an accordion tucked up under one arm and the other about her waist.

Both arms bulged with hard muscles that the sleeves of his T-shirt had been slit to accommodate. Kenyon felt a sudden sinking, as if the wharf had dipped beneath his feet, as if the big boat tied to the piling had begun to reel in its line, tugging the little wharf free of its mooring. He steadied himself and felt the jolt of another pull. It was less a turning of the head than a sideways movement of the eyes that brought him to the source—a big, stocky fellow with a growth of rough beard, his hands dwarfing a fiddle and bow, a stocking cap cuffed above thick brows. He was staring out of red-rimmed eyes, and it wasn't a welcoming look. Kenyon returned it in kind, feeling an instant dislike for the man.

Lennox Callot rattled something incomprehensible, and Sabre swiftly withdrew from the embrace, looking sharply at the burly man. They exchanged brief words, and Kenyon took his gaze away, knowing full well that he was the subject of conversation. He took the opportunity to look over the man whose arms Sabre had just vacated. He was a slightly better version of the other, though taller and thinner, with big, broad shoulders and narrow hips leading to long, jeaned legs. A thatch of jet black hair showed beneath his cap. His jaw, at least, was freshly shaved, and his clothing looked to be clean if worn. Which, he wondered, was Ami Goula, father to that strange child and the "friend" of whom Sabre had spoken? As if sensing his question, Sabre turned a smile on him.

"There's coffee and fish stew," she said lightly. "Will you have some?"

He inclined his head. "Thank you." Deliberately, he stepped into the room and crossed the floor to the table, which had been pushed back against the wall. Lennox Callot sat at one end, his guitar upon his knee, a glass of oily brown liquid at his elbow. He kicked a bench closer to his guest and made the introductions while Kenyon positioned it and sat down.

"Kenyon Ames, attorney, meet my son, Butler." Kenyon made to stand, offering his hand, but Butler Callot was obviously not one to whom formalities meant much. He laid a thick hand upon Kenyon's shoulder, pushed him down on the bench, then caught up his hand in a hardy shake. "Our friend," the old man went on. "And my son's boss, Ami Goula."

Kenyon looked up at the big man, who nodded with barest civility and lifted his chin to position his fiddle. His thick fingers drew the bow across the strings with a jerk. Butler Callot slapped his accordion into place, one knee drawn up, foot set on the end of the bench opposite Kenyon. Lennox Callot tapped out a fast beat and music filled the room, spilling out into the shady bayou. Lennox grinned; Butler Callot laughed out loud, his fingers swiftly working the keys. Sabre brought Kenyon his bowl, then ate from her own while standing against the wall, her toes tapping in time to the music.

It was not the best stew Kenyon had ever eaten. It was thin, with little rice and few vegetables to give it body and an occasional bone mixed in with the bits of fish, but Kenyon's mind wasn't on his food, anyway. He couldn't ignore the feeling of relief that came with the introduction of Butler Callot. Why should he feel glad that it was her brother's neck rather than her "friend's" around which Sabre had wound her arms? Yet, it was a kind of gladness that he felt, gladness and relief. Still... How good a friend *was* Ami Goula? That he was the major source of the Callot's income seemed obvious, but there was a proprietary gleam in those red-rimmed eyes that Kenyon didn't like at all. He reminded himself that he was a man who minded his own business, but that didn't make him like Goula any better. He turned, straddling the bench, the better to observe.

The trio finished one tune, and Lennox Callot, after a sip of his rum, stomped out the beat for another, then paused. "Your man," he said suddenly to Kenyon, "remembered a cousin off to the east of here. He'll be along by turning-in time."

Kenyon lifted his shoulders in a shrug. "I hate to impose on you for another night," he began apologetically, "but this sort of locks us into it, I'm afraid."

Lennox waved away his apology, his spirits obviously lifted by the music, and began once more to tap out the beat. Ami Goula played a quick intro and Butler joined him on the pick up. Kenyon glanced at Sabre, only to find her eyes fastened on her brother's quick fingers. Almost at once, the fiddle dropped out, replaced by Lennox Callot's guitar chording. With surprising speed and agility, Ami Goula set his instrument aside and launched across the room to take Sabre in his arms.

Sabre laughed and hurriedly plunked her bowl and spoon on the table, her feet already moving to the music. Side by side, they skipped forward and back, arms linked. Then suddenly Goula caught her against him, and they went reeling in tight circles about the room. Laughter spilled out of Sabre, getting lost in the music.

It was amazing, the kind and amount of music these folks could get from one guitar and an accordion. It occurred to Kenyon that they were really a happy, inventive people by nature, much more in sync with their element than most others. Yet, he felt no joy at the discovery, no pride or kinship or satisfaction. He felt instead a deep, ugly dread, for these were also desperate people, painfully poor, resourceless, struggling on the very edge of survival. What did they sacrifice? What price did *she* pay for this bare existence?

It seemed interminable, but the tune did end at last, and the dancers fell apart, breathless and exhausted. Sabre shook her glossy auburn hair off her neck, gathering it in her hands between laughter and gasping. Ami Goula reached out with one thick arm and wrapped it about her slender waist, steadying her against him. Nausea swept over Kenyon in a cold, shuddering wave. Even as she slipped free, laughing still, the sickness and suspicion roiled in him, burning in his throat, acidic, bitter, hot. He turned away, catching the old man's eye as he did so. A worried crease was drawn between his grayed brows, and Kenyon understood, in that instant, what a narrow line they walked, what work it took to maintain the delicate balance between subsistence and shame. Ami Goula was the boss. Ami Goula controlled the purse strings. And Ami Goula wanted Sabre. He stood up and walked out the door, the sickness threatening to spill out of him. Behind him the music began again.

They played and danced until midafternoon. Kenyon busied himself, trying to coax the awkward Jeanetta into answering his careful questions. He would have liked to know more about the girl's parents, mother as well as father, but Jeanetta Goula turned out to be no source. She was a rude child and ended his attempt at conversation by sticking her tongue out at him and diving into the canal fully clothed. A few moments later, she scrambled up the anchor line, as agile and quick as a monkey, water pouring from her dark hair in rivulets, the rubber on the bottoms of her shoes squeaking as she ascended the chain. The child went over the railing and jerked around to look at him. He forced a smile and lifted his hand in a limp wave. Jeanetta swept her wet, stringy hair off her face and spat over the port side into the bayou. Kenyon frowned and wondered if they didn't have a bar of soap on that big tub. And why wasn't a child that age in a school?

He had exhausted his concern for Jeanetta Goula by the time the musicians wound down and Ami Goula came out onto the narrow wharf. The "great ape," as Kenyon preferred to think of him, stretched himself, huge arms up and pulled back, thick legs locked in place, his barrel chest puffing out with the deep breath taken in. He glanced at Kenyon, his contempt unveiled, and dismissed him as one might dismiss a bug, then gripped the bow line and hoisted himself aboard, hand over hand, in an incredible display of strength. Kenyon rolled his eyes, telling himself muscles were no substitute for brains. The carefree laugh of Sabre came to him, and he turned away from the towering bulk of the shrimp boat, enchanted despite himself.

He entered the shanty, pausing just inside to let his eyes adjust to the shadow. Brother and sister were seated side by side on the bench at the table, a book open between them.

"And look at the binding," Butler was saying. "It's a quality edition. It ought to bring a pretty penny."

"Not here," Sabre said. "No one cares about quality here."

"No one but you," he countered softly, sliding the book toward her. "And that's just who this is for."

"For me?" She feigned the most joyous surprise. "Ah, brother, you shouldn't spend your hard-earned money on me."

"And then what am I working for?" he countered, before submitting to the arm she wound about his neck.

"To keep body and soul together," she replied gently, "and God love you for it."

Kenyon cleared his throat, surprised to find such strength of attachment.

"What new treasure have we here?" he asked gaily when their heads turned toward him in unison. Sabre lifted the book, twisting around to present it to him.

"Molière," she said. "In French!"

He was taken aback. "You read French, do you?"

"But of course!" Butler declared. "Mamá taught us. She said a body should be on intimate terms with one's ancestry. But Sabre's much better than I am. She's brighter, I think."

"Ha!" his sister protested. "Butler scored 1180 on his college test."

"Oh, and she only scored 1100, little dunce!" He sobered a bit. "It was harder for her, with mother ailing and school so far, but she made us proud, our Sabre, too proud to take the old Gar's money." He said the last to Kenyon's face clearly wanting no mistake made in his meaning.

Kenyon considered carefully his reply. He had here a shabby, unlikely, backwater pair who read French and had scored well enough to be considered for admittance by many of the best colleges in the nation, had they possessed the application fees. Goula, the ape, waited just beyond the door to exploit them, he felt sure. And there was in New Orleans a spoiled, nasty old man with money to burn and an oily great-nephew willing to light the matches. Why, he asked himself, looking at Sabre's patient, intelligent eyes, should Darryl Garrick be the only one to warm himself with such a flame? He struck a laconic pose, its ease belying the careful practice that had gone into perfecting it during his law-school days.

"Vanguard Garrick is your grandfather," he stated simply. "He's ill, and he wants to put his house in order, so to speak. The 'old Gar's money' can be of as much service to you as to your cousin. Why should your pride keep you from that?"

"He can have regrets, can't he?" Sabre argued, her hand tugging at her brother's elbow. "Maybe this is his way of reconciling the family. He's proud, too, and why not? Why shouldn't we give each other a chance?"

"You know why. He turned his back on Mother—and on us."

"But maybe he has regrets."

"Then let him say so. Why salvage his pride at the price of ours?"

"Is ours worth so much more than his?" Sabre insisted. "Isn't the chance at a real future worth something, too?"

Butler was silent for a long while.

"It would have to be you," he said, at last. "We're going out again tomorrow night."

Kenyon pursed his mouth thoughtfully. What would he do in Butler Callot's place? He wondered if he'd have the faith to send off a sister such as Sabre, and then he thought of Ami Goula and knew he would.

"You'll look after her, won't you, Lawyer Ames?" Butler said solemnly.

Kenyon gulped and chose his words carefully. "I'll see her safely delivered and settled in—if she decides to go."

"Ah, a fine point," Sabre said. "It's my decision and mine alone, and I don't want to talk about it anymore, for now!" She made a definite slashing motion with both hands and fell against her brother's shoulder. "Let's make him tell us tales," she proposed, as if contemplating a particularly devious means of torture. Kenyon laughed.

"What stories have I to tell?"

"We shall see!" declared Butler, catching the spirit of Sabre's game. "I will interrogate. Now then, Lawyer Ames, what was it like at college?"

Kenyon soon realized that a deep need to know lay behind their fun and games. Had he always wanted to be a lawyer? Had he known someone special who helped him get into school? Did he have a favorite teacher? Kenyon's laughter was genuine as he answered, his tone only slightly condescending, though he himself was unaware of it.

After a long while, Callot came in from the bedroom, grumbling and rubbing his stomach. Sabre leaped up and began their dinner, spoon bread and fish stew again, only this time, dressed up with spices and thickened with additional rice and filé powder. Kenyon found it quite palatable. It was an enjoyable meal, all in all, despite the fact that Goula and his daughter joined them, the latter still damp from her afternoon swim.

They played dominoes afterward, Kenyon losing handily, until Lennox took up his guitar again and the table went back against the wall once more. Jeanetta found herself a vacant corner and sulked there. Goula played like a demon, his fingers flying wildly over the strings like so many starving little birds in a field rich with seed. Kenyon allowed Sabre to coax him onto the dance floor, and managed to hide the fact that he was an unusually competent dancer. But for every dance he allowed himself, Ami Goula demanded an equal in his silent, forbidding way, and though he counseled with himself against it, that fact greatly irritated Kenyon. He put up with it for some time, thinking as he watched. Vanguard Garrick was a crotchety, self-centered, narrow-minded old curmudgeon, with more money than scruples and a life so far removed from those of people such as these as to make them incomprehensible to him. Van Garrick was all that, and worse. A little thing like Sabre Callot would be defenseless against his manipulations, and yet if she remained here she might well wind up permanently shackled to that great, unkempt ape of a man, Goula.

It was none of his business, of course, and wouldn't make a fig's difference in his own life. Still, he couldn't quite resign himself to leaving her as he'd found her. She might make out in New Orleans, somehow. She was bright, after all, and showed some taste, though her better impulses were no doubt stifled by poverty and isolation. Anything would be better for her than staying here and winding up as Ami Goula's mistress or—worse yet—his wife. Kenyon made up his mind to press for New Orleans as urgently as he dared. He told himself it was the only decent thing to do. She would make out, he told himself. Hell, she could even be right about Garrick. Stranger things had happened. Hadn't they?

Chapter Three

Hot tears came to Sabre's eyes as she took the canvas bag from beneath the narrow bed. It was the very bag with which her mother had eloped, now soft and mottled with age. How ironic that it should take her daughter back to the house and the father from which she had fled that night so long ago. Sabre had known almost from the moment Kenyon Ames had arrived that she must go. She even wanted to go, in a way, and yet it was so hard to think of leaving her family and home behind.

Poor Papá, he was so often in misery. The bones had knit in his back in such a way that both sitting and standing were painful for him. The rum helped a bit, of course, but too often Papá's hand was slow in righting the bottle. And who was going to clean the lamp chimneys and turn the paddle in the old manual-wringer washer out back? She knew there were other, more pertinent questions to ask. Might there be doctors who could help him, and how would they ever pay for their services if they found them? Grandfather's kindness could do that for him, and if not his kindness, then his money. She supposed Papá could wash his few garments in the basin, and come to think of it, the lamps would not blacken too badly because they always kept the wicks low until Butler came home.

Butler. Oh, but she was going to miss him! He was more than brother to her. Since childhood, he had been friend and confidant and sharer of dreams, and for too long now he had been provider and protector, as well. At nineteen, he was that curious hybrid of man and boy. The man she revered and admired, but it was the boy who filled her heart with love and yearning. It was the boy she felt she owed, for he had yielded early to the man who broke his back to put food on the table for father and sister. If ever that boy was to have a chance to dream again, it had to be soon, before he was battered and bowed and beaten down with responsibilities too big to push away. She would miss Butler, but if she could cause love or even pity to warm the heart and loosen the purse strings of Vanguard Garrick, then Butler Callot would realize his dreams. She would miss him less, knowing this.

She gathered her clothing and her courage at the same time, trying not to think of the things that had been said the night before when she had called them together and announced her decision. Her father had warned that she was bound to be disappointed. Vanguard Garrick would not accept her, he had said, but in the end he gave her his blessing. Butler, as Butler would, had held himself responsible for her decision and begged her not to go on his account, saying that he had found his place in life and was content with it. She had known better, of course, but with Ami there, she didn't want to say so.

Ami was offended by talk of college and change. He wanted no life other than what he had, and he resented any implication that he was ignorant or unenviable. He truly didn't understand that there could be more to life than the bayou and his boat. Oh, Ami understood comfort and personal ambition. He knew desire and lack. What Ami could not conceive was that anyone could want anything other than what he wanted himself, and what Ami wanted just then was a woman to warm his bed and order his house and handle his child—and the woman he wanted was Sabre Callot. That made her going problematic for Butler in more ways than one. Besides, she truly had no desire to add insult to Ami Goula's list of irritations.

It wasn't as if Ami was a bad man, after all. Many a girl in her class at school had found Ami Goula an enticement. He worked hard and was ambitious in his way. He was big and confident, a natural leader, if in a brutish manner, and frank about his needs and desires. In fact, Sabre would have looked on him as something of a savior if only she hadn't found him so boring and oafish. It wasn't his fault that he could talk of nothing but the price of shrimps and a man's capacities for work and drink and... Well, there were some things, to his credit, of which he didn't speak to a woman not yet his wife, except indirectly, anyway. But there were also some things a man such as Ami didn't accept in silence, like the sudden departure of the woman he wanted, for one. It was Ami who had said the things Sabre didn't want to remember, things that her brother and father wouldn't, things she had thought herself but had discounted with a desperate mixture of hope and logic.

Deliberately, she began to stow her belongings in the canvas bag, forcing her brain to assign each a purpose. Unfortunately, these worn, mundane things were not enough to fully occupy her. Her hands shook and folded and stacked what she was to carry away with her, but as she worked, the words she hadn't wanted to hear seemed to be whispered into an unprotected inner ear.

"You're abandoning your father, and the man so ill he keeps half drunk to blunt the pain. Your brother has enough to worry about. If you leave the old man alone, he'll have more to worry about than ever! You want your brother to be so crazy with worry he doesn't watch his work and *he* gets hurt?"

Her hands slowed, as the terrible guilt came back to her. And the guilt didn't stop with her father and brother, Ami had made certain of that.

"And what about my Jeanetta? I thought you were going to spend time with her, talk to her about the things a father cannot. You know, some people are lucky to have two parents 'til they're grown. You think my Jeanetta wouldn't like to be you, eh? You think you've had it so bad?"

Sabre looked at the things she had accumulated. They were well-worn, but they were clean and mended and useful. They were all she had ever had, but Ami was right. Life had not been so bad for her, not as long as her mother had lived. Somehow, as long as Gamelin had been with them, they had not seemed poor. They had not known hopelessness. They had not feared what tomorrow might bring.

Her father had aged ten years since her mother had died, and Sabre felt she had, also. But even that was better than what Jeanetta had known, for Jeanetta had never really known the care of a mother. Perhaps, thought Sabre, that was why the child couldn't like her. If only Sabre could believe that would change. But no, she couldn't expect to be Jeanetta's mother without being Ami's wife, and Sabre couldn't convince herself that such was her destiny. Try as she might, she couldn't believe that Ami Goula was the husband for her. If only she could say honestly to Ami that she wanted no part of him, but how could she when it was through his hand that the money came to feed her family?

Sabre wished that Kenyon Ames could understand that. But Kenyon Ames couldn't understand how one person could be beholden to another for the very necessities of life. He couldn't see that it was Ami's goodwill that kept her brother employed and food on their table. Ami didn't have to choose Butler. There were plenty of men who would have gladly taken his place, but how could Kenyon Ames understand that, raised as he was in a big house, with money and cars and influential friends? He had never known what it meant to depend on the goodwill of another. Still, she was grateful for the way he had argued in her favor and a little awed.

"Sabre is an intelligent woman," he had said, refuting Ami's contention that she would be lost in the city. "She can adjust. She can master. There are risks, of course, but aren't there always? As men, we've each chosen our own risks. I believe Sabre's entitled to the same freedom."

It was as if he had looked deeply into her heart and read her most private thoughts, bringing them finally to light. In that moment, he had become a symbol of what she wanted and, in her heart of hearts, felt she deserved, while Ami had become the thing she most feared: ignorance. It had seemed so simple. One's way offered the chance of a better life and the knowledge with which to achieve it, while the other's denied such knowledge existed and touted the needs of everyone but the very person whose life was in question.

The choice was more muddled now, with the sorrow of leaving and the fear of failure. Would Grandfather give her a chance? Did he miss his daughter's children and secretly yearn for them? Was it fair of her to hope for his kindness and generosity, to leave father and brother in that hope? She was wavering, going back and forth, when Kenyon popped in.

"Ready?" he asked, his tone inviting and cheery. "If we set off soon, we can be in New Orleans by afternoon and at the Garrick house by early evening." He rubbed his hands together as if savoring the thought of a banquet, and she felt certain he had noticed, somehow, her growing ambivalence. "Ever been to New Orleans?" He leaned against the wall and folded his arms. There was the kind of twinkle in his eye that had been there the previous day when she and Butler had gotten him talking about his college career. Already buoyed somewhat, Sabre moved her things aside and plopped onto the foot of her narrow bed.

"Once, when I was very small, my parents took us to see the Mardi Gras parades. It was during Mardi Gras, you see, that my father first saw my mother. She was riding on a big float in an elegant costume, and there were many people packed into the street. Papá had climbed onto a balcony in order to see more clearly, and just as Mamá came by, a man rushed out and chased him away. He jumped and landed right at Mamá's feet, and that is how they met. He had no money and no place to sleep, but he stayed in the city, and when he came back to the bayou, Mamá came with him."

"So they took you to see the city of romance, did they?"

"Well, I don't remember very much. I was very small. What I remember best, in fact, was Butler crying and Mamá creeping away to feed him and missing all the excitement, and Papá saying it was all right really because Mamá had seen so many Mardi Gras and even been to the balls."

"Would you like to go to a Mardi Gras ball, Sabre?"

She laughed, for it was a silly question. "But of course!"

"Perhaps you will," he said, "if your grandfather is still active in his krewe." But she couldn't imagine such a thing, not even if her grandfather had maintained an active membership in his exclusive club, and so she pursued her original question again.

"What is it like, New Orleans?"

He smiled to himself for a moment, and she did so like the rapturous expression on his face. "She's unlike any other city on this continent," he told her. "By day she's almost a slattern, but even her tatters are so elegant that you can't quite wish them away, and by night she's a temptress, so glowing and worldly and rich she takes your breath away! She's French and Spanish and Caribbean, aristocratic and common, and never, ever boring!''

Sabre hugged herself, entranced and dreamy. *New Orleans*. The very name seemed to promise life and excitement and success.

"Come now," Kenyon said, rousing her to the moment. "She's waiting."

He went out, and Sabre got up to finish her packing, new determination in her, though just why she couldn't say. There was something about Kenyon Ames that made her feel . . . hopeful. She shook her head to keep from remembering the feel of his mouth on hers, and crammed her canvas bag with the stuff of her life. When she came to the dress, however, she immediately paused again.

It was her very best dress, and she was fond of it in a way that only a woman with one good dress could be. She had made it from an old but well-preserved dress of her mother and worn it to the spring *fais do-do* at the church in the swamp that last year of school. How she had danced that night! It had been her first grown-up party, and everyone had said she was the prettiest girl there. She'd kept a part of that feeling over time, and protected it by wearing the dress only on important occasions. She would wear this dress to meet her grandfather.

The dark blue fabric had body and gloss. It felt like silk in her hands. She had cut the neckline daringly low, had second thoughts, and had filled in with wide white lace that stood up against her neck in the back and overlapped in the front. When she'd bought the lace and a narrow belt to cover with fabric taken from the skirt, the clerk had thrown in a card of pearl buttons as a *lagniappe*, a kind of reward for making the purchase. The buttons "riched up" the dress, to her mind, and she had been so proud to replace the original flat, navy buttons with the shiny white ones. The belt had taken only three of the sharp, narrow pleats from the skirt, leaving it still quite gloriously full. All that fabric in one skirt! It felt utterly extravagant. The short, puffed sleeves were quite feminine, especially since she'd added white cuffs salvaged from the yoke of a shirt outgrown by Butler. This was her best, though secondhand and remade, and she would wear it on this most important day in her life. Confident, she folded the dress and laid it gently atop the slightly down-in-the-heels white patent-leather pumps she'd received from her parents on the day of her high-school graduation.

Those shoes murdered her feet, but she didn't care. She'd wear them gladly, to make the correct impression. She'd read about first impressions and their importance, and she was determined to make the most of her first meeting with her grandfather. Perhaps if he saw how serious she was, how important this was to her, it would make a difference. She wanted him to feel honored, to know she had given thought and care to her appearance, and she was counting on those murderous pumps and the good blue dress to create the right feeling.

She closed the bag and took it by the handle in one hand, reaching with the other for the net holding the collection of favorite books she had chosen even before the blue dress. With the sum of her worldly possessions in her two hands, she went out to meet the moment.

Her father was sitting at the table, a grim look on his face. Her brother sat upon the cot, his elbows on his knees, hands clasped, eyes upon the floor. He looked up as she entered the room, but the best smile he could give her was a strained, straight line across his face. Ami leaned in the doorway, one foot on the wharf, his thick arms folded against his chest. He scowled at her, clearly angry still, and this gave her the strength she needed to toss her head and lock it in her most stubborn pose.

She went quickly to her father and kissed his bent head, promising, in a soothing voice, to think of him every night and pray for his health. Her brother stood, as she went to meet him, and wrapped her in his solid arms. He was very close to tears, she knew, but she made herself laugh and shake him gently.

"Take care of him," she said, jerking a nod toward their father. "And take care of yourself." He nodded mutely and rubbed his nose. She spun away, hurrying now before her composure crumbled. She ducked her head and murmured a farewell to Ami, but as she attempted to slip past him, his strong hands came out and caught her. She clutched her bags and felt herself hauled against him. Gritting her teeth, she allowed him to kiss her. She had never found this pleasant, but today she found it completely revolting. As his mouth ground against hers, she sought a way to endure, and it came to her in the memory of another mouth and other hands upon her body.

Just for a moment, she felt traitorous for thinking of Kenyon Ames, but the guilt passed in a wave of resentment. Firmly, she pushed away from Ami, eyes glaring a silent message of rejection; then she gathered herself together. Behind her, at the end of the wharf, Kenyon Ames cleared his throat and coughed. The lazy, cynical smile on Ami's face told her that he had created the scene he had intended and was content to let it be. Masking her relief in an expression of utter calm, she turned and walked to the waiting boat.

Piroux sat in the stern, his hand upon the tiller. Kenyon took her bags and lowered them into the boat, his face a bit too composed to hide his amused disdain. She wondered if it was the books or the old canvas bag, but told herself it didn't matter. Lawyer Ames was doing a job, and soon his part in this would be finished. She would do well to remember that. Who did he think he was, anyway, looking down his handsome nose at her? She pushed his helping hand away and climbed down into the boat unaided, seating herself in the center, her possessions about her. He climbed into the bow, cast off, and straddled the seat, his smile welcoming this time.

"Next stop, New Orleans," he said cheerily. She was shaking so badly she wondered that the boat didn't rock, but she didn't want anyone else to know that, especially not Kenyon Ames. She held herself rigid as the outboard motor sputtered to life and the little boat pulled slowly away from the pier. She waved a farewell to whoever stood watch over her departure, but in truth, she couldn't bear to look back, so though her hand wagged back and forth enthusiastically, her eyes were tightly shut.

It was harder to go away than she had imagined, and she couldn't help wondering if she had made a mistake almost before the little boat had carried her out of sight of the shanty on the bayou. So many emotions were warring within her that it was difficult to settle on one feeling and hold onto it. Irritation soon came to be clearest among them.

"I suppose you're anxious about meeting your grandfather," Kenyon said after some minutes filled with only the noise of the engine.

"Should I be anxious?"

He blinked at her, looking distinctly uncomfortable. "Well, it's bound to be a little awkward. I—I thought you understood that."

Of course she understood that. Her nerves were just on edge. She made herself smile and nod. "I'll need to change before I see him," she said almost offhandedly.

"No doubt," he replied, and she instantly felt insult in the words.

"Are you saying I'm not fit as I am to see my own grand-father?" Anger churned inside her.

He opened his mouth, then closed it again, took a deep breath and gave her a blunt look. She saw in it the decision to be honest, and knew she didn't really want or need to hear his answer.

"I'm saying that your grandfather is a tough, opinion-ated, aristocratic old man," he told her flatly, "and he'll regard those comfortable jeans you're wearing as field clothes. You show up in them, and chances are, he'll throw you out on your ear. So I hope you brought something else."

"Of course, I brought something else!" she retorted, less insulted than worried. She knew she'd better get a grip on these feelings, and set her gaze on the horizon, effectively ending the conversation. She tried not to think, but her brain just wasn't cooperating. What if she got there and he decided he didn't want to see her? What if he wouldn't let her in the house? Where would she go? What would she do? She felt the beginnings of real panic. Clenching her hands into fists, she made herself breathe deeply and slowly until the feeling passed away. She was on her way to freedom of choice, she told herself. She had a new life waiting for her— and for Butler and for Papá and even for Grandfather—if he would only open his heart to her. But even if that didn't happen, New Orleans was her only hope, her only real hope, and she had to remember that, whatever came. Finally, feeling much more her real self, she took a book from her net bag, slid down onto the bottom of the boat, got com-fortable, and was soon far away in thought and feeling content.

Kenyon couldn't quite make himself unaware of her. It was guilt, he decided. Obviously, she was having second thoughts. He'd known it, sensed it earlier, maybe because *he* was having second thoughts. All that he'd said the night before, the eloquent speeches, the lawyer's tricks of persuasion, had contained no genuine element of reality. It was one thing to say she would make out all right in New Orleans; it was another thing entirely to know it. Why hadn't he stayed out of it? he wondered. Was Ami Goula truly a fate worse than death?

He looked at her, sitting there in the bottom of his rented boat, wearing faded jeans that fit like a second skin, her shapely legs crossed and drawn up to support the book she was reading. He had never seen such intense concentration. If he'd had just a fraction of that much concentration at her age, he could've taken the bar a year sooner. What a shame she'd never had the opportunity to use those powers for anything more important than entertaining herself. If she had gone to college, her whole life would be different now. He wouldn't have found her living in a shanty on the bayou, peddling used books door-to-door and letting herself be pawed by Goula. Maybe she'd have had a real chance with Garrick.

He sighed and raked his fingers through his hair, trying to tell himself that whatever happened in New Orleans wasn't his problem. His job had been to find her and her brother, notify them of Garrick's intent, determine if there was any interest on their part, and report back to Garrick with his findings. He knew perfectly well that he'd overstepped certain boundaries by urging her to take the action she had. He wanted to believe that she would have been here in the boat anyway, that he hadn't influenced her unduly, but he couldn't forget that he'd argued in favor of her coming with him to New Orleans, that he'd promised her brother he'd assist her, that he'd painted this exotic picture of the city for her. And he couldn't forget that he'd kissed her, or how he'd felt when Goula had done the same.

It would work out, he told himself. She was a charming girl. She had intelligence. She could learn. It wasn't as if she didn't have someplace to go, after all. Garrick House was open to her—for now. He suddenly got a mental picture of the trio awaiting her there: Van Garrick, with his manipulative arrogance; Mallory, with her dour, possessive scowl and rapier tongue; Darryl, with his rampant greed and oily ethics. Next to that unholy alliance, Sabre Callot was a true innocent, a sacrificial lamb. Merciful God, what an idiot he'd been!

He tried to think of what to do, how to protect her and salve his conscience. She would need a friend. He had a feeling the Garrick houseman could be of assistance, but would that really be enough? He doubted it. Well, he knew lots of people in New Orleans. There was bound to be someone who could serve the purpose, someone who could guide her, warn her, encourage her. He racked his brain, listing and discarding name after name. Who was he kidding, anyway? The very people he knew were the people least likely to accept her. His heart was pounding much too heavily. He felt like a kid caught in a lie. But that was stupid. He hadn't done anything, really, except encourage a lovely, young woman to go after an inheritance that was legitimately hers. What she did now wasn't even his business, let alone his responsibility.

Compassion was one thing and responsibility another. Was it his fault the Callots lived as they did? Had he forced Van Garrick to disown his daughter? Did he encourage Gamelin Garrick to run off with a poor yokel from the bayou?

He felt better once he'd absolved himself of responsibility in Sabre Callot's life, and he made a silent resolution to adhere to the new policy. She was a good-looking but totally unsuitable woman, whom he'd kissed in a moment of weakness. He felt sorry for her. Who, with a beating heart, wouldn't?

Somehow, he was able to maintain that thought for the remainder of their trip through the bayou. Once they moved into real swamp, however, it wasn't necessary as Piroux needed him to take up an oar. His complete concentration was required to help get them through the thickest portion of the undergrowth without losing it. By the time they got to the launch point, he was hot and sticky and tired, and all he could think about was getting a cold drink and a shower.

Sabre, on the other hand, seemed as fresh as a daisy. As they beached the small boat on the gravel embankment near Piroux's neat brick house, she closed her book, stowed it away, and stretched the kinks out of her muscles like a lazy cat. The moment the boat ground to a halt, she got up and stepped out. Kenyon sank down on the manmade embankment, wet to the knees and aching between the shoulder blades and up the back of his neck. Piroux unloaded the canoe, piling their few articles on dry land. His wife came out the back door of their house, the screen snapping shut behind her with a bang. Piroux smiled and trudged toward the house. Within moments he had reached the back porch and was giving his wife a bear hug of greeting. They went inside together, Piroux calling out for them to follow.

Kenyon just wanted to lie back and close his eyes. Such a trip this had been, but a couple of hours from now he'd be back in New Orleans. *They*, he reminded himself. *They would be back in New Orleans.* Sabre seemed to be thinking the same thing.

"What now?" she asked, hands on her hips. Kenyon shrugged.

"I'll change into dry shoes and socks, get a drink, stick my head under a cold spigot, comb my hair, pay Piroux, then we'll get in the car and go."

"Ah," she said. "Makes sense."

He squinted up at her, the position of the sun making it difficult to see anything but this cloud of wildfire around her head. "What did you think we were going to do, stick our thumbs out and hitch a ride?"

She laughed nervously. "I guess I didn't think about it. It's all so strange, you know. And I seldom go anywhere I can't get to by boat."

"How did you and your parents go, do you remember?"

She nodded, and he could feel her smile. "*Oui*, I remember. One does not forget such a ride! We met a friend of Papá's—I can't recall where—and he had this old pickup truck. It hardly had any paint—a little blue, a little gray, a little rust." She laughed and came down to his level, kneeling in front of him. He could see her face clearly now, though the sun still made a halo of fire of her hair. "Mamá and Butler rode up front with the man and his wife. Papá and I rode in the back with all these children. There must have been five or six of them, and in my mind they were all about the same age, though, of course, they weren't—for they were all brothers and sisters, you see. Anyway, we rode in the back of that truck all day, it seemed, the wind blowing in our faces and whipping our hair about, and Papá played the guitar for us, and we sang at the top of our thin voices until we were all hoarse. I remember every time we went over a bump we'd all come up in the air and down again so hard!" She laughed, a little girl once more, and Kenyon couldn't help thinking how lovely she was, how wholesome.

"Well," he said, dusting off his hands and struggling to his feet, "our trip will be less eventful." He rotated one shoulder, groaning aloud. It occurred to him that he'd been sore since he'd started this trip. Sabre came quickly to her feet.

"Are you hurt?"

"Naw, it's all these darned oars."

"Ah. Gets you right between the shoulder blades, doesn't it? Here, I can help. Bend over."

"What?"

"Bend over. Go on. As far as you can. That's right. Now, bend your knees a little. Arms out in front."

"Oh, great," he said to his kneecaps. "I'm speed-skiing on gravel."

"What was that?"

"Speed ski— Uh, never mind. Could we get this over with, or are you just trying to make me look like an idiot?"

She laughed and pushed his head down until his chin was against his chest, and held it there. "Now," she said, "slowly straighten up. Come on. Not too fast. There. Now your head." She removed her hand. "Slowly. Take it all the way back. Good."

He lifted his head and pressed his shoulders back. Miraculously, the tension in his muscles was almost gone. He put a hand to the back of his neck, chuckling.

"Well, that's a new one on me," he admitted.

"It won't work unless someone else holds your head down," she told him. "I don't know why. It's just not the same."

"A buddy exercise, huh?"

"I guess so."

"Well, thanks. I'll remember that."

"I should be thanking you," she said, her voice silky and low. Suddenly, he was very much aware of her physical presence. Her nearness brought a lump to his throat and caused stirrings in other parts of his body he didn't dare contemplate. He swallowed.

"I, um, haven't done anything I haven't been paid for."

"Oh?" Her tone held laughter. "Did my grandfather pay you to kiss me?"

He heard a rushing sound in his ears, like water pouring into his head, and he was having a devil of a time keeping his hands to himself. He swallowed again. "No. I mean . . . of course not."

"I didn't think so," she commented teasingly, and he was so achingly aware of her face turned up to his, that pretty, little mouth just inviting him to take it, that he was having a hard time thinking.

"Uh. W-we . . ." He shifted his weight, trying to appear casual. "We should, um . . ."

"Go?" she suggested helpfully. He latched onto that word like it was a life raft.

"Right! Oh, yeah, you're right. We should go." He managed to take a step to the side, and as she turned to follow, he managed another. It was only when he'd gotten some distance between them that he realized he was trembling. But he didn't dare stop—until they were all the way to New Orleans.

Chapter Four

The dress was a disaster. He saw it the moment she stepped off the elevator. He'd taken her to his hotel because he knew the concierge well enough to ask to borrow a room for an hour or so and because after that long, tense car ride, he needed a cold shower and a calm moment to get himself in hand. He was well beyond second thoughts now. These were deep, dark fourth and fifth thoughts he was having, thoughts full of disaster and foreboding. She was a fascinatingly beautiful woman, voluptuous, striking, sexy almost beyond endurance and so definitely out of her element in such a sophisticated city as New Orleans she literally drew stares.

Oh, hell, he said to himself. *The Garricks are going to have this kid for lunch, and if they don't, their upper-crust friends will.* And it was all his fault.

He berated himself for not having had better judgment, and tried to smile at the same time, for she was weaving her way through the hotel lobby toward him. It was all he could do to keep from wincing.

The dress was too small for her. She looked like a child in an outgrown hand-me-down. The skirt was absolutely the wrong length. It should have been shorter or longer. As it was, it hit about half an inch above the top of her knees, calling attention to the fact that she wasn't wearing stockings and should have been. The lace around the neckline was grotesquely frilly, while the dress itself was prim and tailored. The cuffs on the slightly puffed sleeves looked childish and yellowed and were not the same color as the lace at the neckline or the buttons on the bodice. The shoes were run-down, and she walked as if they hurt her feet.

At least she'd done something fetching with her hair. She'd pinned up her lush auburn locks on both sides in two sleek, tapered rolls. The back had been brushed to a high gloss and left hanging smooth and long. The local effect was truly charming, even chic, but when coupled with that infantile dress the overall impression was absurd. *Accentuate the positive,* he told himself, but he cringed at the very idea of presenting her to Vanguard Garrick in that getup.

On the other hand, what was he to do? He could be brutally honest, tell her she looked ridiculous, and insist she allow him to buy her a presentable outfit, if he had the time. Unfortunately he'd already called up Garrick and told him to expect them within the hour, and to make matters worse, he'd allowed his friend to come and pick up the car. Having returned it a full day later than he'd promised, he hadn't been in any position to ask to keep it. Without time and extremely convenient transportation, there wasn't a darn thing he could do about a change of clothing for Sabre, in which case it would be nothing short of cruel to let her know how unsuitable the dress was. All he could do was hope the Garricks were more charitable than he judged they were.

He rose and managed a smile when she joined him, but he couldn't keep himself from glancing around the room to see just how much attention they were receiving. Feeling guilty, he made himself target his gaze on her face, and immediately thought what a lovely face it was. A touch of mascara and a bit of blush would make her competition for any cover girl. As it was, it was one of the most naturally beautiful faces he'd ever seen, and when one thought of the body beneath it . . . But, no, that wouldn't be wise, at all.

Her own eyes were averted, and he could tell that she was uneasy. He longed to reach out to her, to reassure her, but doing so seemed not only dishonest but ill-advised. He was suddenly fatigued, utterly exhausted, but he couldn't do anything about that, either. He was beginning to feel helpless.

"I like your suit," she said timidly.

He thanked her, though it was just a plain blue one worn with a pale yellow shirt striped in maroon and a maroon tie bearing a single yellow stripe outlined in navy. Nothing special, at all.

"I like your hair," he told her as warmly as he could manage. She actually blushed a dusky crimson beneath the healthy, light olive tone of her skin.

"*Merci*," she whispered, looking so tiny and frightened and lost that he put his arm around her before he could even think. He had to do something, anything to help her. If only there was someone who could smooth the way, so to speak. If he could just . . . Theo. That was the ticket. He actually started with the realization. "What?" she asked, concern darkening her golden eyes.

"Oh, I . . . have to make a phone call. Gosh, I'm sorry. It won't take a minute." Hurriedly, he helped her into the chair he'd just vacated, then crossed the room to the bank of phones mounted against a marble wall. He picked up a receiver and punched in a number. Three rings sounded in his ear before Theo answered.

"Garrick House."

Just the sound of his voice reassured Kenyon. Theo was a likable old gentleman, the epitome of the old-fashioned houseman. Kenyon wondered how he'd managed to put up with the Garricks all these years.

"Theo, this is Kenyon Ames."

"Mr. Ames, so good to hear from you again."

"Thank you, Theo."

"If you'll hold just a moment, sir, I'll buzz Master Vanguard's room."

"No, don't do that. I wanted to speak to you, Theo. I want to ask a favor of you."

There was a slight pause. "Me, sir? Well, certainly, if I can help in some way."

Kenyon pinched the bridge of his nose, searching for the correct words. "It's about Miss Sabre Callot."

"Miss Callot? I'm afraid I'm not familiar with the name, sir."

"Sabre Callot is the granddaughter of Mr. Garrick."

"Miss Gamelin's daughter, sir?" He sounded positively thrilled at the prospect.

"The same."

"Good land o' Goshen!"

Kenyon wondered what Theo would say when he saw her. He pinched his nose again.

"I assumed Mr. Garrick would tell you he was expecting guests."

"He did that, sir, but if I'd a-known it was Miss Gamelin's girl . . . ! This is good news, sir!"

"I'm glad you think so, Theo. It does make it easier for me to ask you this. The thing is, you see, she's . . . I don't know quite how to say this. She's, well, Miss Sabre's not like Van and Mallory. God knows, she's not like Darryl. What

I mean is, she's not going to fit in very well, I'm afraid. Theo, she's going to need an ally, a strong, diplomatic ally.''

"I think I understand," the slow drawl came back. "And you needn't worry too much, sir. I was particular fond of Miss Gamelin. Naturally, I'll want to look after her daughter as best I can."

Kenyon sighed audibly. "Thank you, Theo. I'm in your debt."

"Not at all, sir! Why, the very idea of it. Now you come along with Miss Sabre at your convenience, sir. I, for one, will be mighty glad to see her."

Kenyon felt better after that conversation, but only slightly. There was only so much, after all, that a servant could do.

He rejoined Sabre only long enough to explain that it was time they were on their way. Taking her elbow, he escorted her swiftly across the lobby, down a series of carpeted steps, and across the marble floor to the Canal Street door.

"My bags," she said, but he propelled her forward firmly.

"They'll be sent to you." It was bad enough that she had to show up in that dress. He didn't intend to compound matters by dragging along a battered canvas bag and a fish net. This way, only Theo had to see how shabbily she came equipped.

They crossed the street and walked down a couple of blocks to St. Charles Avenue. The early evening weather was perfect, with that diaphanous sunshine peculiar to New Orleans and a gentle breeze coming from the direction of the river. The streets were busy in that languid Crescent City way, with offices still disgorging a few well-heeled occupants and taxis screeching their brakes.

There were a few street people mingled with the business crowd, the ragged, colorless clothes and bundles of odds and ends a sharp contrast to trim suits and expensive valises. A group of Oriental youths in jeans and T-shirts pushed past them, bouncing on the balls of their feet and laughing as they strode along. A black couple came toward them. The man wore a calypso shirt and slender black pants and carried a guitar. The woman was garbed in a very short ruffled skirt, turban, high heels and off-the-shoulder blouse. She carried a tambourine and a small leather bag, which Kenyon knew contained several kerosene torches and a lighter. He'd seen them before on the corner of Conti and Bourbon. The man played the guitar and juggled the lit torches; the woman sang and danced. Both were really good. He'd given them five dollars only a few nights ago, and others in the sizable crowd had also contributed generously. Sabre watched them closely, clearly mesmerized. Kenyon smiled to himself, thinking what fun she would have on tacky Bourbon Street when the real eccentrics came out to play.

He scratched that thought and concentrated on the ordeal to come. It occurred to him that the real nightmare was likely to be Sabre's alone. He could only imagine what snide remarks Darryl Garrick would make, what vicious asides Mallory might utter in that supercilious tone of hers. And the horrible part of it was they'd likely be right in the majority of their judgments. Sabre was simply not up to the level of society the Garrick family enjoyed. Why on earth hadn't he realized before what it was going to be like for her? He was in a torment of guilt and worry, and the fact that Sabre trembled within his grip did not give him confidence.

They stood for several minutes while Kenyon tried to hail a cab, but it was a busy time of day, with plenty of regular customers competing for service. A crowd had gathered on the far corner of Bourbon and Canal, telling him it was about time for the trolley to arrive. Grasping her hand, he led her toward the crosswalk.

Her shoes were obviously killing her feet, though she made no complaint. They reached the corner just as the light turned in their favor, and they hurried across with a dozen or so other pedestrians, several of whom joined the crowd waiting for the trolley. Wondering how long Sabre's feet could endure, he hoped they could get on the first car to arrive.

He noticed that a couple of other women had hopped up on an empty newspaper stand, and he didn't hesitate to motion Sabre over and give her a boost up. She was surprisingly light, and he found himself remembering what she'd felt like pressed against his body. He immediately withdrew and shoved his hands down at his sides. She folded her own hands primly, her bare knees pressed firmly together in a ladylike pose. He wondered if she was thinking what he was thinking, but quickly banished the thought, telling himself he had no business kissing her then and no business thinking of it now.

He tried to think of all the *safe* women he knew: Janet, the stewardess; Alicia, the hostess at his elegant club; Andy, proprietess of a chic women's clothing shop; Shannon, Houston's sexiest lawyer, what a liberated woman she was! They were all delectable women, good-looking, sensuous, well-educated, broad-minded, careful. Not one of them, however desperate, would allow a cretin like Ami Goula to come near her. He felt angry when he thought how that great, rusty ape had handled Sabre. How could she bear him? How could she even think of... But this was not the exercise he'd intended. Still, it served to remind him why she was here, and he knew suddenly that he couldn't have left her as he'd found her. He had done the only thing he could, given the circumstance, the only thing his sense of compassion would allow.

Looked at that way, his actions seemed not only understandable but laudable. What else could a man do, after all, except what his conscience demanded? If he could just figure out what to do about her now.

A number of thoughts sprang to mind. He didn't have to go back to Houston right away. There was nothing pressing him, at the moment. And he need not stay on at the hotel indefinitely. He had a standing invitation to use the apartment of a friend who was currently abroad. Since it was in the French Quarter, one had to get used to the traffic on the street below, of course, but there was a top-of-the-line compact-disc player and an impressive collection of music to help drown out any background noise. Then there was that courtyard, unusually quiet and serene, and a stunning woman across the way. Maybe that was what he needed right now to regain his perspective. In that case, there were several women in town who wouldn't mind spending an evening or two with him. One, in particular, came to mind.

He smiled to himself, thinking he'd found the perfect solution. He could satisfy his conscience and solve his problem at the same time. Now all he needed to do was find a way to get Sabre into one of the finer dress shops in town. With a few clothes and some subtle coaching, not to mention Theo's support and input, she might be able to hold on until Garrick made his decision. And if it went against her, what then?

He would cross that bridge when he came to it—if he ever did. She might surprise him. Given a little time to adjust, she might well take her own life in hand and come up with her own solutions. Why, of course, she would. She wasn't an imbecile, after all. She just needed a little time and a show of support. In fact, he might be blowing this whole thing out of proportion. She could turn out to be much more capable than he imagined. He decided to put off any decision for a couple of days, telling himself he was too tired and keyed up to think straight.

The trolley arrived. The driver killed the clattering engine, and people began pressing for entrance as others escaped out the other end. Kenyon dug in his pockets for the fare, realized he didn't have any change, and resigned himself to forking over two whole dollars rather than the dollar-twenty that was the total of both fares. Sabre hopped down off the stand, and Kenyon dragged her along behind him as he fought his way through the crowd. They squeezed on board, and he thrust the bills at the attendant, who took them without comment. All the window seats were already full, so he placed her on the aisle next to an old man with a long, gray ponytail, and sat down behind her, next to a young man with a ponytail and a black fedora. She glanced nervously over her shoulder, which he patted reassuringly, and her little hand with its ragged nails came fluttering up to meet his. She ought to have a manicure, he decided impulsively, and a pedicure and one of those sumptuous facials women were always talking about. Her nerve apparently bolstered, she let her hand fall to her lap, and he took his away from her shoulder, telling himself it was going to be all right. This wasn't going to be the disaster he'd imagined.

The trolley engine sputtered and the little train car lurched forward. A moment later they actually began to move around one corner and then another. Soon they were heading southward at a leisurely pace approaching six miles per hour, but that was only between stops, which came every block or two. Twenty-five minutes later, they passed General Taylor Street and began the approach to Napoleon. Kenyon took a deep breath, preparing himself for the coming meeting. He could, quite simply, do nothing else—but he felt far more miserable about that than he should have.

Sabre gulped air and held it. Her feet were pinched and chafed, and her head was beginning to hurt. Maybe she should take out the pins in her hair, she mused, but she knew she wasn't going to. Kenyon liked it this way. She could tell he didn't like the dress, and that made her feel self-conscious, indeed. She saw well enough that it wasn't fashionable streetwear in New Orleans, but surely *Grand-père*'s view would be less—the word was "hip," wasn't it?

She let out her breath and straightened, pulling herself very tall from the waist up. She was Sabre Callot, she reminded herself, daughter of Gamelin and Lennox Callot, good folks both. She had nothing to be ashamed of. Quite the contrary, she had much to be proud of. She relaxed just a bit and smiled at the elderly gentleman on her left. He inclined his head in a signal of respect, and it was then that she first noticed the long, gray ponytail lying upon his shoulder. She quickly looked away, unsure whether to be shocked or amused. She decided on amused, but she could feel herself trembling beneath the conscious decision to relax. Her stomach began to twist in knots.

She was too preoccupied with herself to be curious about her surroundings. Kenyon was sitting behind her; she couldn't forget that. She felt dependent on him, and instinct told her that was unwise. Where was it he had said he was from? She knew his distinctive drawl and the way he had of putting extra syllables to words sometimes ought to tell her, but she couldn't quite remember. It didn't matter, anyway. Wherever he was from, he was bound to be going back there shortly. That thought made her feel quite small and alone. She wished he'd put his hand on her shoulder again, and as if reading her thoughts, he did so. Then the next instant he was standing beside her, making her realize they'd reached their stop.

She felt as if she were in a dream. Everything seemed to move so slowly. The old man spread out a bit as she stood, and she felt as if she couldn't get out of his way quickly enough. Kenyon's hand closed on her elbow, and he stepped back a bit to allow her room to move into the aisle. She pushed and pulled herself and finally managed to get into the narrow space between the seats, then slowly turned to face the rear of the trolley car. Concentrating very hard, she slogged her way toward the door, stepped down, stepped down again, and stepped down once more to the uneven ground. It was grassy here in the median. The thick growth tickled her feet above the tops of her shoes as her clunky heels sunk into the spongy ground.

Kenyon was right with her, his hand resting lightly on her back just above her waist. She marveled at his patience as they moved slowly toward the street. Each step was an agony, but she closed her mind to the pain and concentrated on moving ahead, on lifting her foot and putting it down again, shifting her weight, and beginning again on the other side. Behind them she heard the scraping sound of the trolley door closing, and then, minutes later, it seemed, the splut-splut-splut of the engine. They reached the street. She felt the impact of the cement curb on her toe. Pain radiated through her foot and spread up her leg. At first she thought the collision of toe and curb had something to do with his hands appearing at her shoulders, with the closing of his fingers on her upper arms, with the resistance to her movement and the resulting backward flow. But then a car, a sleek blur of black and beige, whisked past her, and suddenly she was aware, shuddering and clinging to the arms that held her.

They spoke, or rather he did, but though she heard the sounds, she didn't hear the words. She was looking at a building on the far side of the street, a huge, massive house with massive brick columns and wide verandas and walkways that curved gently through a lush, green yard overhung by a pair of massive oaks. It was the biggest house she'd ever seen, as big, it seemed, as the hotel from which they'd just come. Her heart, suddenly, was in her throat, and she turned first in one direction then another, taking in her surroundings: the shaded street split by a grassy median lined with trolley tracks, the big houses, each unique and looking like a historical landmark, schooled lawns, ornate fences of blackened iron and sturdy brick. She knew from her reading that she was looking at a legacy from another century; even the trolley was a part of it. Only the sleek autos flowing past and lining the streets were from the present, and yet they, too, were foreign to her, so that the scene was all of a piece to her and she was suddenly terrified.

Kenyon waited for a break in the traffic, then propelled her off the curb and across the street. She knew by the force of his grip that he was upset with her for nearly stepping in front of that car, but it just didn't matter at the moment. All that mattered was this strange, new world in which she found herself; this foreign, frightening world where she would never belong. Her feet were killing her, and she fastened on that as a way to stave off the panic she felt rising within her, but in three steps she was hobbling and unable to go on.

"Take them off!" Kenyon commanded the instant they reached the sidewalk. She gratefully did so, bending down, one foot raised, then another. The cement felt warm and solid beneath her, sandpaper-rough against her bare soles. The freedom from pain was exhilarating, so much so that she felt almost normal when he took her hand in his. "Come on," he said, pulling her along to the corner and across a side street. Her feet were flying, her shoes flopping together as they dangled from her left hand. And then they stopped.

Kenyon stood staring up at the white, colonnaded mansion, but Sabre could not see past the ivied brick wall. A little way up was an arched wrought-iron gate, and Sabre walked toward it, her hand still in his. She stopped beside it, stepped forward and pressed her small face between the ornate bars. There were sixteen columns, in all, eight up and eight down, with wide shuttered windows beyond and a tall center door painted a clean, verdant green. Patterned, cast-iron railings set off the second-story terrace, while the downstairs veranda was distinguished by brick red tiles. These were also used on wide steps bordered by a walkway that was hedged by sculpted shrubs perhaps eighteen inches high.

Beyond the main house and the west wing, which jutted out to the side, stood an old carriage house, its green roof looking prim in the waning sunshine. Every double door was closed, and the graveled drive had been swept free of tire tracks. Brass lanterns were affixed to support posts beneath the eaves; one or two of them were already beginning to flicker faintly in the shadows. An apartment had been built over the far west end of what was now a garage, and a light switched on in a corner window as Sabre watched.

Kenyon reached for the rope of an eight-inch-wide brass bell mounted on the wall to the side of the gate. He gave the clapper three hard swings, making the bell ring out in a clear, dignified tone. Without further announcement, Kenyon pushed down on the latch, and the gate swung smoothly open. Sabre held her breath, and found suddenly that she couldn't move, but the paralysis fled the instant Kenyon slipped past and tugged at her hand. She followed him gratefully, giving herself over to the awed survey of her surroundings. There was a trim, disciplined jungle hiding beyond the six-foot brick wall, presided over by a stately old oak and a pair of saucy palms.

A rope swing, undulating gently, hung from one limb of the oak, and she remembered her mother's voice saying, "I had the most magnificent swing, when I was a girl, and I used to dream that my beau would entertain me there, and the hem of my gown would trail in the dust as I swung to and fro.'' But the bare spot beneath the swing where dirt had been ground to dust by little-girl feet was gone, covered over by grass coaxed and nursed by a gardener.

For one heady moment, Sabre felt an urge to rush to that swing and bounce upon the seat where her mother had bounced, to drag her bare toes through the green, slick grass at last and feel at one with that other person her mother had been, the carefree girl, the happy, giggling, innocent child from this other world. A car door slammed somewhere, and the moment disappeared abruptly. She and Kenyon went up the curving walk and climbed the steps.

Sabre halted at the top and set down her shoes. Balancing herself with one hand on a classic Greek Revival column and the other on Kenyon's strong shoulder, she forced one foot and then another into the tight, confining spaces of her shoes. Her heels were raw and her toes pinched mercilessly, but she knew somehow that this was the least of her problems. Banning thought, she screwed up her courage, shoulders lifting and dropping with the intake and storage of air tasting faintly of oil. She primped her hair, lifting it away from her shoulders to plump it, and patting the tight roles above each temple into neat symmetry. She was vaguely aware of a headache, but it registered a zero on her scale of concern, at the moment.

''All right,'' she said, and let out her breath in one long stream from her nostrils. ''Let's do it.''

''Sabre.'' The urgent sound of Kenyon's voice caught at her like plucking fingers, and she turned on the balls of her feet to face him. His mouth worked at words that wouldn't make themselves audible, then closed.

''It's all right, Kenyon,'' she said, unconsciously using his given name, but he shook his head.

''I don't think I've prepared you very well for what you're going to find in there.''

"Don't be silly," she said, her voice sounding surprisingly calm even to her own ears. "I've heard stories about Grandfather and Aunt Mallory since I was a child. Aunt Mallory was horrid to her, and Grandfather was dictatorial and unreasonable and—"

Just then the door opened, revealing a slender, fair man with features a bit too sharp and hair that just missed being limp and somehow still managed to look stylishly sleek. His Adam's apple bobbed as he laughed, the sound coming up from deep within his narrow throat. Sabre took it for pleasure and smiled at him, expecting a civil greeting if not a real welcome.

"Hello," she said, raising her hand and stepping forward. "I'm Sabre Callot."

The man gave her a blatant once-over and shook his head.

"Good God," he said to someone behind him. "She looks like she was dressed by the Salvation Army."

Sabre was stunned, appalled, deeply wounded. Her hands went to her face, her mouth a small, round O. She felt Kenyon at her side, a strong, protective presence, and suddenly she desperately needed him to hold her, to hide her from this cruel, arrogant stranger. Her breath catching in a strangled sob, she whirled and reached out for him. His strong, willing arms came around her. His broad shoulder made a pillow for her head. She was safe for the moment, steadied— but only because she couldn't see his face, the anger, regret and horror. It was the look of a trapped man who might have saved himself, might have avoided the very thing he most feared, but too late realized that he was hopelessly, desperately lost.

Chapter Five

Of all the ill-bred, ignorant, hateful things to say!" Kenyon stated.

"Oh, my, yes, it was a terrible slip of the tongue. My apologies, cousin. It was just that ghastly dress. Caught me off guard, you see."

"Somebody ought to punch you in the nose, Darryl, and I'm just the fellow for the job!"

"Well, that's a lawyer for you! Ever heard of assault and battery, old boy? I understand they get rather serious about that sort of thing."

"Not as serious as I'm going to get, if you don't curb your nasty impulses."

"Here now!" said a feminine voice. "I'll not stand for this. Darryl, since you have apologized, please withdraw now."

"As you wish, Aunt Mallory."

Sabre made herself straighten. Blinking back tears, she turned to face her great-aunt. Mallory was a tall woman, with chin-length hair too dark and too straight for her age. She wore a mustard yellow dress with a dropped waist and a softly flared skirt. Her nails were painted a pearlescent beige and she wore a ring bearing a single, enormous, emerald-cut topaz. Her expression was one of unmistakable disapproval, but Sabre had expected this. It was the outright attack she hadn't expected, the blatant insult. Everything her mother had ever said, everything her mother had ever been had spoken of gentility and well-mannered subtlety. Neither precluded cruelty nor snobbery, but they did allow one to face such unpleasantness with dignity and poise. Sabre lifted her chin in a show of determination, and quietly turned to give Kenyon a small, grateful smile.

"Are you all right?" he asked gently. She nodded.

"Aunt Mallory," she said, turning to offer her hand. "I'm pleased to meet you."

Mallory all but sniffed, her spine ramrod-straight, her eyes narrow slits that gave away nothing. She put a flaccid hand into Sabre's. "Do be kind enough to wait a moment before coming up. I'll need a moment to prepare him. Theo will show you the way."

An elderly gentleman appeared. As Mallory turned and walked away, he took her place in the doorway. "Hello, Miss Sabre," he said in a kindly voice. "Welcome to Garrick House."

He was a spare, compact individual, with hair as white as his coat and eyes as black as his skinny bow tie. His trousers were black, too, with a razor-sharp crease that broke against the instep of a pair of shiny black shoes. Sabre thought he looked positively regal. She nodded in what she hoped was an equally regal manner.

"It's nice to meet you, Theo. Are we related?"

"Oh, my, no." He chuckled. "I'm the houseman, but I've been here so long I feel like family. Won't you come in? Mr. Ames, so nice to see you again, sir."

He cleared the way for them, but Sabre couldn't quite make herself go in until Kenyon stepped forward and took her elbow in his hand. He smiled encouragingly and nodded, and together they crossed the threshold into Garrick House.

It was immense, with a ceiling that soared two stories and marble flooring veined with gold. Sabre couldn't quite believe her eyes. There were gilt-framed mirrors and vases of flowers resting atop a trio of ornately carved little tables. The focus, of course, was a wide staircase that swept upward in a delicate curve, its wooden risers polished and gleaming. She thought of the hotel where Kenyon had taken her and how impressed she had been, but no more impressed than now. She kept looking for all the people. It seemed ridiculous that only three should be in residence, four counting Theo.

Thinking of Theo, she turned and gave him a smile, unsure of how one was supposed to treat a houseman. It occurred to her that he was a servant but the idea seemed truly foreign. She didn't want to offend.

"Did you know my mother?" she asked.

His smile was quick and wide. "Oh, yes, miss, from the day she was born. What a pretty thing she was, too, and you just like her."

Sabre's smile widened. "*Merci*. Ah, thank you. Thank you very much."

"You're very welcome, and if I might suggest it, miss, don't pay too much attention to Mr. Darryl. I think he's feeling a bit insecure, just now."

"And well he might," put in Kenyon.

"As you say, sir," replied Theo, a decided twinkle of mischief in his eye. "Now, if you'll follow me, please." He started up the staircase. Sabre climbed it with her eyes, coming at last to the massive chandelier overhead. It was not lit at the moment, and yet it sparkled and gleamed like a honeycomb of unbelievably large diamonds. She took a deep breath and walked forward, then halted, aware suddenly that Kenyon had not followed.

"Aren't you coming?" Her voice sounded desperate, even to her own ears, and she straightened, chin up, shoulders square. Kenyon nodded.

"Sure. Sure, I'll come. I rather think Van expects me."

She could not disguise her relief and only hoped she could find a way to repay his kindness. With that thought in mind, she held her hand out to him. He took it and gave it a squeeze.

"Up we go."

Theo had halted about a third of the way up, waiting for them to catch up, then went on at an easy, steady pace. Sabre looked around her, smiling at the paintings on the wall and stealing glimpses at the main hall below. When they came to the landing, Sabre took one last look over the banister before following Theo down a hallway to the left. Her grandfather was in one of those rooms. Could he hear their footsteps? Did he anticipate, with excitement, his first sight of his granddaughter? She was trembling, and her feet hurt terribly, but she couldn't think of that now. They walked past one door and then another, halting finally at a third. Theo opened the door and stepped aside.

"After you, miss."

Kenyon released her hand and nodded encouragingly. She faced the door, thinking, *He's going to hate me*. But she'd known that was a possibility all along. Screwing up her courage, she stepped inside. It was not what she'd expected; it was just a small room, with a narrow sofa and a couple of chairs.

"This is the small sitting room," Theo said, in his gravelly voice. He indicated a door to their left. "That's the large sitting room. Master Vanguard's private dining room is to the right, and this is the bedchamber." He walked straight ahead and rapped on that door with his knuckles, opened it a bit, listened and, satisfied, opened it wider. A wave of hot air hit Sabre full in the face, and she heard Theo's rough voice saying, "Mr. Kenyon Ames to see you, sir, and Miss Sabre Callot."

"Well, get them the hell in here, man, and get on about your business!"

Kenyon shot Sabre a look that clearly said, "No, his bark is not worse than his bite." Then he stepped quickly through the door, his hand held out for her to follow. She appreciated that little gesture of deference and solidarity, and it gave her the lift she needed to see this thing through. She put on her calmest face and strode into the bedchamber with her head held high, her hand finding Kenyon's as if of its own accord. Together, they walked into the center of the room, while Sabre quickly took in her surroundings.

It was something of a letdown after the opulence of the entry. The bed was a hefty four-poster, its wood dull and dark. The drapes were closed and made of heavy, dark red velvet trimmed in gold fringe that had definitely seen brighter days. The carpet underfoot was a similar shade. The part of it that wasn't worn was almost colorless, as were a trio of armless chairs placed about the room. A large, forest green armchair sat before a fireplace where a black screen protected it from the flames, which crackled on the grate. Beside the chair was a small desk, turned sideways. There were stacks of papers on it, each weighted with a palm-sized stone, and a pair of bifocals with cheap, black plastic frames. The only other furnishings were a pair of mismatched nightstands flanking the bed and a row of five ugly, metal filing cabinets along one wall. Everything smelled of wood smoke and camphor. Most disappointing of all was the little, old gnome propped in the center of the bed.

He looked quite feeble, with long, bony hands and a bald, cadaverous head atop a spindly neck. He wore silk pajamas at least one size too large, so that the sleeves had to be rolled up to expose the skeletal hands. Yet, despite the feebleness, he had a feral look about him; a cunning, alert look that made the thin smile upon his mouth seem sinister.

"You're right. She does look like her mother," he commented to Mallory, who stood at his bedside, nodding. He waved her forward, and Kenyon released her hand with an encouraging little push. She took one step. "I understand your mother is dead," he stated matter-of-factly.

Sabre nodded. "Nearly three years, now." She kept her voice quiet and low. "I don't think my father will ever recover."

"We will not speak of your father," Vanguard Garrick ordered summarily. "Now, what of your brother?"

Sabre lifted her chin, loyalty to her father putting sharp words into her head, but Kenyon stepped forward and dropped a hand on her shoulder, a clear warning. She'd already opened her mouth, but closed it again to reformulate. "Butler," she said, pausing to take a deep breath, "is as fine as any nineteen-year-old doing the dirty work on a shrimper can be."

Vanguard Garrick snorted. "Well, that's not very fine, is it?"

Mallory clucked her tongue, head wagging. "I suppose it's the best he can do."

"It's the best he can do *under the circumstances*," Sabre said a bit too loudly, and there came another brief squeeze from Kenyon's hand. She was trembling but no longer with nervous dread. She clamped her mouth shut, playing it cool.

Vanguard Garrick pursed his lips thoughtfully. "That may be so," he said dismissively. "We'll not debate it now." He linked his bony hands atop the dark red bedspread over the slight protrusion of his belly. "Tell me about yourself, Sabre. What do you do with yourself there in the swamp?"

"Mostly, I read," she began, but the telltale pressure told her to stop, and the next moment Kenyon Ames had taken over the telling of her story.

"Your granddaughter is quite the entrepreneur," he said in a surprisingly conversational tone. He dropped his hand and strolled toward the bed. Reluctantly, Sabre followed, wondering what he would say next. "She's really rather enterprising," Kenyon went on. "There aren't many business opportunities in the bayou, as you might have guessed, but Sabre has managed to establish herself as a business-woman."

"And in what business are you established?" Garrick asked, his question clearly targeting her and not the lawyer now standing at the foot of his bed.

Sabre thought quickly. "I sell books," she said simply.

"On a small scale, of course," Kenyon went on. "A rather unorthodox arrangement, in fact, but profitable." He smiled at her, but above the curve of his mouth, his blue eyes were telegraphing caution. Sabre swallowed hard and tried to be still. "Unfortunately," Kenyon was saying, "the possibility of expansion is nonexistent. The market is so small, well..." He shook his head as if to say the matter didn't rate discussion. "What counts, of course, is the drive demonstrated and the intelligence."

"What counts, Mr. Ames," said her grandfather stonily, "is what I say counts." He looked down his long nose at Sabre. "Where did you get that awful dress?" he asked, then waved away any reply. "Never mind. I don't want to know." He lifted an eyebrow at Kenyon, then shifted his attention once more to Sabre. "All right. Tell me something about yourself."

Sabre inclined her head in a shrug. "Wh-what did you want to know?"

"Well, were you comfortable in the swamp? Did you live well?"

Sabre considered her answer carefully. "I lived in the bayou, not the swamp," she said at last. "No, we didn't live very well, not in the way you mean." This answer seemed to please the old man on some level, so she grew bolder, stepping up right to the foot of his bed, her bare knees against the dry wood. "We are very poor, *Grand-père*," she explained evenly.

"Grandfather," he corrected. "You will call me Grandfather." Stung, she bowed her head. "Go on, go on!" he ordered impatiently.

Sabre took a deep breath. "We're very poor. All the extra money I made with my books went to food and medicines and Mother's wake. We still owe the church two hundred dollars for that, but it was a grand wake, I promise you." He looked put out, but she went on in a smooth, satiny voice. "I was happy in school, and so was Butler. So much so that both of us regretted graduating. We'd have liked to go on to college, you see, but as we are such poor people... Well, we work at what we can. With Papá... That is, since Butler and I are the only ones able to work, it's been quite a strain. But then I have to say, Grandfather, sir, that we've had a good life in another way. We've had lots of love, and it's a poverty of that which makes people truly unhappy, is it not?"

For a moment, Sabre felt quite proud of herself. She felt certain that she had put the interview on the right footing, at last, and perhaps had opened a door for a deeper kind of communication. She wanted to be honest with him, after all, and she wanted to bring to his life something from the riches of her own. She felt for the first time during that whole long day that they might be able to reach an accord in spite of everything. But Vanguard Garrick pursed his lips and hitched an eyebrow at his sister, who lifted the back of her hand to her forehead and rolled her eyes.

"As emotional as her mother," she said.

"Young woman—" Garrick leaned forward in his silk pajamas, ignoring his sister's response "—don't think you can sway me with sentimental babble. I disapproved of your mother's attitude, and of your grandmother's before her. If the latter had died some years earlier, I might have been able to make a real Garrick out of your mother, but I made an unfortunate match, you see, and the result was an unfortunate child, who in turn made an unfortunate match."

"And another unfortunate child?" Sabre said hotly, her shock and disappointment and the hours of dread combining to get the best of her. "I wanted to think that the years and the illness had softened you, opened you to what you closed when you banished my mother. I wanted to think I could comfort you, love you."

"You want my money," he stated flatly. "As to my health, I've no doubt I'll live too long to suit you—whether you inherit, or not. So be it." He groped for something on the bedside table, found a large, rumpled handkerchief, and brought it to his mouth, which he wiped. "Now," he said, folding the handkerchief and thrusting it away from him, "we may form an alliance of sorts, once we get to know one another, but understand me. I'm more concerned with whether or not you can live up to the standards of a real Garrick. You don't have to be a genius, but you do need character and taste and grit. That's what I'm looking for."

Sabre listened as he went on talking about forbearance and tradition and position, his tone thin and unemotional. Sabre thought of her brother working on Ami's shrimp boat, of her father suffering in silence, of her mother's serene and loving smile. "Character," he said, "and taste and grit." He didn't begin to know his subjects. How could he, living in this huge house, with servants and money and complete security? She felt herself hardening, felt the strength flow into her limbs and stiffen her spine.

"Do we understand one another?" he asked at last.

Sabre lifted her chin and tossed her hair. "Perfectly," she said. "Should I measure up, you'll give me money and position, but nothing else, certainly not anything as emotional as love. All right, Grandfather, whatever I can get, I'll take—gladly."

The old, dark eyes widened. They were a muddy brown, she noticed, and the whites were yellowed and etched with red. He began to laugh, feebly at first, and then stronger until finally he was barking, his bald head falling back upon the pillow.

"Well, by God, she's honest!" And he laughed on, delighted to have reduced her so quickly to greed.

Sabre glared, determination stoking her courage, then politely took her leave and turned away. She stalked from the room, surprising herself with her composure. She closed the door, then realized Kenyon had stayed behind. She no longer knew what to think or do, and the pain in her feet was suddenly agonizing. She sank onto the small divan, the anger that had sustained her draining away. She bent over and removed her shoes. Her feet were swollen and throbbing. The heels and toes were red and raw and already beginning to puff with blisters. She looked at them and at the hateful white shoes, and all at once tears were rolling down her cheeks. Oh, what was to become of her? And how could she have expected to love that awful old man in there? But she wouldn't cry. She simply wouldn't give in to it. Quickly, she wiped her face and took a deep, cleansing breath.

The door opened, and Kenyon came in. He gave her a tiny, sympathetic smile and came to sit beside her on the divan. Sabre bit her lip.

"I ruined it, didn't I?"

He shrugged. "I don't know, to tell you the truth. I think he liked your spunk. It's hard to tell with him. I thought you handled yourself pretty well, though."

"I shouldn't have come," she said, taking no comfort in what he'd said.

"Well, that may or may not be true," he told her, "but you did come and now you have to make the best of it."

She sighed and swung her bare feet, skimming the colorful rug. It was patterned with flowers and birds.

"It's not what I thought it would be, you know? I mean, the house..." She lifted her arms to encompass this one little room. "I didn't know there were houses like this. I didn't know there were hotels like that one today, but I figured it's a very big place, so many people, so much money. But for one man to own a house like this..." She shook her head, speechless. For several moments, neither of them said anything, then she shrugged. "I haven't been thrown out. I guess I'm staying, eh?"

"It doesn't have to be that way," he stated gently, but she shook her head.

"No, I couldn't go back. Not yet. It would mean—" She bit off the mention of Ami Goula. She couldn't bear to speak of him, somehow.

"I understand," he said, and she had the feeling that he really did. He was a pretty amazing fellow, this Kenyon Ames, good-looking, smart, educated, compassionate. She could have gone on, but it didn't seem wise. It wasn't as if he was going to be around for her to depend upon, and she already knew from experience that dependence could be its own trap. She decided to make her peace and be done with it, with him, while she could.

"You've been very kind," she said softly. "I want you to know how grateful I am, especially as I was so touchy this morning."

"No, you weren't so..." He chuckled and rubbed his ear. "Well, all right, maybe you were a little uptight. It's understandable, all things considered. Besides, you helped me get the kinks out after all that rowing. That's a good trick. I'll have to remember that next time I...row."

She smiled at him. "You'll need help. Someone has to hold your head down. Don't forget."

"No, I won't forget," he said, and he was smiling, too. "Well, I'd better be going." He got up, and she came instantly to her feet. They didn't hurt so much now that they were free of those awful shoes.

"I, um, guess you'll be going back to—" It came to her suddenly. "Houston."

He rubbed a hand on the back of his neck. "Well, I don't know. I mean, maybe not right away."

"Oh?" She couldn't help feeling hopeful about that.

He nodded and explained, "I have several friends in the area, and since I'm here I'll probably, you know, hang around. See some people."

"Of course, *oui*, I see what you mean." She took a deep breath and a calculated risk. "Well, since I won't be seeing you again, I'd better say goodbye now." She stuck out her hand and smiled. He started to take it, then, to her delight, declined.

"Listen, I'll be around. I'll drop by before I leave, and that way, if you should need anything, you can...call."

She lifted up on tiptoe, suddenly feeling quite exuberant. "That's wonderful. Thank you. I'll look forward to it—to seeing you, I mean."

He cleared his throat, suddenly antsy. "Okay. All right. Well, I'd better get out of here. Theo will probably be around in a minute. If I see him, I'll send him in. You just take it easy now, and if I can help, you just call the hotel. It's room number 2929."

"Twenty-nine twenty-nine," she repeated. "I'll remember."

"Right. Well, goodbye, and ... Goodbye."

"*Adieu, bon ami.* Godspeed."

He nodded. His hand found the doorknob, then he was gone, and the door was closing behind him. Sabre stood in the middle of the little room, feeling warmed and hopeful and renewed.

"I'll see you again," she said softly, and the door opened once more. She skipped back, thinking he had returned, but it was Theo's white head that came into view.

"Miss Sabre, I'm to put you in the west wing. How'd you like to stay in your momma's old room? It's pretty much as she left it. Lots of her things still there." He looked down at her bare, bruised feet. "Don't you fret now. We'll find something around here you can wear that won't eat up your little feet like those others."

Sabre felt her face color, but why should she be embarrassed? He was so kind and understanding. She wondered how he could be, working around here all these years.

"Thank you, Theo. Is it all right if I walk barefoot, then?"

He pushed the door open wide and grinned at her. "You just try to put them things back on, miss, and old Theo'll give you what for."

She laughed and stooped to pick them up. "Very well, Theo. Lead the way."

"If you'll permit me, Miss Sabre." The houseman made a dignified bow and took the shoes, tucking them neatly beneath his arm. "This way, please."

She laughed. He certainly did know how to make one feel pampered. It wasn't so bad, really. With a friend like Theo—and a friend like Kenyon—a person could endure a lot. The hallway carpet felt cool and soft beneath her bare feet, and without Darryl or Mallory or Grandfather to mar her enjoyment, the house felt welcoming and safe. She enjoyed just looking at it, discovering all its little nooks and crannies along the way, but the thought that occupied her, the question she kept asking herself, was when was she going to see him again? When would Kenyon, dear Kenyon, come to call?

Sabre lay on her back on the elegant bed and twisted the mint green spread in her hands while staring up at the flowered canopy.

"I will not cry," she whispered fiercely. "I will not cry. I will not cry." But the next moment tears welled in her eyes, and she rolled over, burying her face in the ruffled pillow.

Damn that Mallory! How could one person find so much fault with another?

"Don't slump, Sabre. You're not sitting on the bank of the river with a hook in the water."

"My dear, if you persist in 'hunkering down' over your food, I shall have to ask you to eat in the kitchen."

"Honestly, Sabre, you carry yourself like a streetwalker. Have you never met *anyone* with the proper deportment?"

Criticism had also been leveled at her "vulgar" accent, her hairstyle, her "lack of taste" and her "incessant chattering." She was either too much underfoot or "skulking around like a thief," butting in where she didn't belong or "exhibiting a conspicuous lack of interest." Nothing she did was ever right. Nothing she said was ever credible. And her looks! Had anyone ever presented such a poor picture?

"Sabre darling, surely you aren't going to the park looking like *that*? You'll be mistaken for a vagrant."

"Poor dear, if only we could do something about the unfortunate color of your skin. Oh, and don't answer the door of Garrick House in those old pants. They went out of style twenty-five years ago! But then you wouldn't know that, would you?"

It was all Sabre could do to keep from shrieking, especially when Darryl "defended her."

"Don't be so hard on her, Auntie. They've probably never heard of *Vogue* in the bayou."

"Come now, we can't expect poor Sabre to participate fully in life at Garrick House. Her heart's still in the bayou, isn't it, *chèrie*?"

The point seemed to be that he belonged and she did not, but she didn't dare publicly challenge the veiled assertion. To do so would have been to admit it had credence. Instead, she spent every private moment she could snatch in her room, reminding herself why she was here and embroidering the fantasies that made separation from home and loved ones bearable.

As if Mallory's acerbic critiques and Darryl's oblique insults were not enough, she also endured Grandfather's litany of complaints. He called it "getting acquainted," but to Sabre it was an exercise in biting her tongue. By Grandfather's account, life had dealt him a ghastly hand of cards. His wife, though beautiful, had been an emotional leech, a constant embarrassment and a spendthrift. She had turned Gamelin into a flighty, whiny child, completely unable to appreciate him as a father or a businessman. In addition, his own brother had been exceedingly jealous of his prominence and wealth, and this naturally had led to harsh words and finally a complete break. Added to these family failings were a wide-ranging selection of dishonest business partners, scheming underlings, false friends and unfaithful lovers. It was a miracle of will and shrewdness, he claimed, that he'd managed to prosper in such a bankrupt environment. There was no telling what he might have done if he had not been so handicapped! The worst of these handicaps was, of course, his daughter.

"I expected her to understand me," he'd said. "Blood of my blood, and all that. A man can be excused for expecting his only child to embrace his standards, to try to please him. But she made it plain that she wanted no part of the world I'd built for her. I had to face the fact that my opinions meant nothing to her. And so I lost her."

He genuinely seemed to have no understanding of how deeply the break had affected his daughter. He couldn't seem to think of her suffering and rejected, out of hand, the idea that she could have genuinely loved Lennox Callot. As far as Van Garrick was concerned, his daughter's marriage was a rejection of him as her father. Period.

No word of contradiction or argument was allowed during these "visits." More objective viewpoints were rejected, out of hand. He claimed the right to translate his life as he saw fit, having "endured" it. Sabre quickly learned the futility of argument, but she did feel that her grandfather enjoyed her company. When she ignored the potential for debate and concentrated on pleasant small talk, his mood would often lighten. He would laugh and banter and allow her to tease him. But the moment she began to speak about her parents or her brother, his patience became strained and he would quickly "tire." She wondered how much longer she could go on like this, and her eyes filled anew when she realized it had been merely a matter of days.

If it were not for Theo, she didn't think she could go on. He seemed her only friend, and she sought the comfort of his company as often as possible, joining him as he worked and listening to him chatter. He talked often of Gamelin, and his memories were so different from her grandfather's that she had to wonder if they recalled the same person who had become her mother. The endearing, delicate girl whom Theo described seemed to have little in common with the disobedient, unfeeling one of whom her grandfather spoke and the strong, content woman she had known. The incongruity, though bothersome on a certain level, gave her a clearer understanding of what her mother's youth must have been like.

Still, she liked it better when Theo talked of his little great-granddaughter, Mary Jill, whom he adored and promised to introduce to Sabre at first opportunity. She sounded like an adorable child, and Sabre looked forward to meeting her. Sometimes she even seized upon that future meeting as a reason to stay. Today, however, thoughts of Theo and his Mary Jill only made her wish for home and her own family there. Suddenly, she wanted desperately to return to them.

But it was too soon to admit defeat. She was made of stronger stuff than that. As much as she loved the bayou, she had no future there, none apart from Ami Goula, anyway, and neither did Butler or Papá. She sat up and took a very deep breath. The tears began to subside. She pulled a tissue from the box on the bedside table and dried her face. Next to the box lay a slip of paper with a phone number on it. She picked it up and turned it over in her hand. Many times she had been tempted to call, but she didn't want to seem frivolous or dependent. Still, to hear a friendly voice other than Theo's . . .

She bit her lip and slipped off the bed to pad silently across the floor to the small desk by the window where the pink telephone sat. It was a rotary dial, but she didn't find that at all strange. She sat down on the upholstered chair and lifted the receiver. Very carefully, she dialed the number and waited. The first ring had barely sounded when a smooth feminine voice came on the line and announced the name of the hotel. Sabre stated clearly that she wished to speak with Mr. Ames in room number 2929. The operator asked her to wait, then came back several moments later with the news that Mr. Ames was out. Would she like to leave a message?

"Oh, yes, please. Say that Miss Callot phoned but . . ." She didn't want to worry him. It wasn't as if he could really do anything. She put a hand to her cheek. "Well, maybe not. No, I've, uh, changed my mind. No message. Thank you, anyway."

She hung up, feeling deflated and foolish. Perhaps he'd thought better of dropping by to see her. Or maybe he was just so busy with his friends. Yes, that was probably it. And she didn't want to make a nuisance of herself, after all. She opened a drawer in the desk and laid the slip of paper in it for safekeeping. There was a book inside. She lifted it out and read the binding. She remembered her mother speaking of this novel. It was as if she'd discovered a little piece of her mother, something tangible with which to soothe herself.

She carried the book to bed and snuggled down between the pillows. And the reality of Garrick House was held at bay for a while.

SILHOUETTE GIVES YOU SIX REASONS TO CELEBRATE!

MAIL THE BALLOON TODAY!

INCLUDING:

1.
4 FREE BOOKS

2.
A LOVELY 20k GOLD ELECTROPLATED CHAIN

3.
A SURPRISE BONUS

AND MORE!

TAKE A LOOK...

Yes, become a Silhouette subscriber and the celebration goes on forever.

To begin with we'll send you:

4 new Silhouette Romance™ novels — FREE

a lovely 20k gold electroplated chain—FREE

an exciting mystery bonus—FREE

And that's not all! Special extras— Three more reasons to celebrate.

4. FREE Home Delivery! That's right! We'll send you 4 **FREE** books, and you'll be under no obligation to purchase any in the future. You may keep the books and return the accompanying statement marked cancel.

If we don't hear from you, about a month later we'll send you six additional novels to read and enjoy. If you decide to keep them, you'll pay the already low price of just $2.25* each — AND there's no extra charge for delivery! There are no hidden extras! You may cancel at any time! But as long as you wish to continue, every month we'll send you six more books, which you can purchase or return at our cost, cancelling your subscription.

5. Free Monthly Newsletter! It's the indispensable insiders' look at our most popular writers and their upcoming novels. Now you can have a behind-the-scenes look at the fascinating world of Silhouette! It's an added bonus you'll look forward to every month!

6. More Surprise Gifts! Because our home subscribers are our most valued readers, we'll be sending you additional free gifts from time to time — as a token of our appreciation.

Chapter Six

Kenyon glanced at his watch, his irritation growing with each passing second. Why did some women think it was completely acceptable to be late? He knew Karen Cromier well enough to know she was always late, and he knew her friends well enough to know they always excused her, but why should they? All right, she was a most attractive woman, generous, affectionate, delightful company, and drop-dead sexy, but did that give her the right to leave a man hanging somewhere between boredom and insult? Then again, he'd known when he'd called her and made the date that she'd be late. Why did it seem so damned personal now? Because he was out of sorts, of course, and because he'd spent the past several days marking time rather than really doing something—anything—meaningful. He should have gone home to Houston. How many times had he told himself that?

He snatched up his highball and took a long drink. The volatile liquid went down bitter and sharp. He sat the glass on the gleaming copper bar top and pushed it away. The bartender approached questioningly, but he shook his head and the man turned away. Despite himself, he pushed up his cuff and looked at his watch again. Twenty-four minutes after seven. Where was the woman? He pushed the thought away, and another instantly took its place. What was going on at Garrick House? Was she having dinner? Locked in her room? Alone? Crying? Was Mallory even now grinding away at her, saying awful things in veiled phrases with double meanings?

He gnashed his teeth, feeling guilty and stupid and responsible. Why had he even called? Why couldn't he have left well enough alone? The operator had said she'd given her name but no message. He could have ignored it, passed it off as boredom or some insignificant impulse, but no, he had to call, and she had sobbed into the telephone receiver, sounding heartbroken.

"How silly of me," she'd said, "to cry on your shoulder like this, only I don't know anyone else, and poor Theo's sort of caught between, you see. But I really shouldn't be so sensitive, and I'm not going to be." She'd sniffed loudly and sighed. "There. Now. All done. I feel much better." And her voice had trembled when she'd said it.

Stop it! he told himself, passing his hand over his eyes. It made no sense to worry about Sabre. She wasn't his responsibility, after all. She'd made him feel sorry for her, but that didn't justify his depth of concern. If only he hadn't kissed her, if only he hadn't let himself get caught up in her life, he wouldn't feel so wretched. Sabre Callot was not his problem, after all. He hadn't stuck her out there in the bayou with just the barest necessities for survival. He hadn't created that nasty old ogre of a grandfather for her, and he hadn't forced her to come here and live with the Garricks. And the fact that he wanted to sleep with her had nothing to do with anything.

She's not your sort, Ames, so forget it. But forgetting Sabre Callot had proved a difficult endeavor. Difficult, perhaps, but not impossible. He reached for his glass and took another drink. Where was Karen, his cure? He drained the glass and signaled the bartender for a refill.

Another six full minutes passed before Karen made her entrance. It was, as usual, worth the wait. She swept through the hotel lobby and into the bar as if she owned the place, a sequined jacket trailing from her fingers, her bare shoulders tanned and smooth. The little black dress she wore—emphasis on the *little*—was strapless and practically backless, with a very mini, form-hugging skirt. Sheer black stockings, stiletto heels, and long diamond eardrops completed the ensemble. The effect was heart-stopping, but it was her hair that really captured his attention. It swung about her hips in wild, stylish, strawberry blonde disarray. He forgave her her tardiness instantly.

"You look fantastic!" he said, coming to his feet. "But what have you done with your hair. It's a foot longer than the last time I saw you."

She released that throaty laugh, kissed him and settled onto the bar stool he had just vacated. "It's a new weaving technique," she confided quietly. "It's like a permanent fall, a hairpiece. In this case, many hairpieces."

He shook his head, more amused by this small disclosure than surprised. Trust Karen to be right in the thick of the hottest trends. He marveled at the hair, again. It looked so natural, so Karen. Probably cost her a mint. He dropped a kiss on her bare shoulder and took the seat next to her.

"All right, beautiful, what will you have to drink?"

"Ooh, something exotic. I feel decadent tonight."

This was good news. He laughed. "Darlin,' you are decadent. Why do you think I called? You're just what I need tonight." He flagged the bartender and ordered the most ridiculous concoction he could think of. By morning, he told himself, he wouldn't even remember Sabre Callot. Yet even as he formed the thought, an unbidden image flashed before his mind's eye—uncomplicated Sabre with her glossy, lustrous, rich auburn hair falling down the center of her back. The vision sobered him, but he laughed at something clever Karen was saying and was pleased at the natural sound of it. They chatted a moment, and she made one of those guaranteed-to-excite gestures that only she could get away with. It was a little thing, really, just the pressure of her hand upon his leg, but he was delighted that his body responded the way he expected it to—and appalled at the relief he felt.

He moved closer to Karen and dropped an arm around her bare shoulders. She purred something about it having been too long. He replied that he'd meant to call sooner, added that he was in town on business, and said how very, very glad he was to have this time to spend with her. She turned the charm up all the way, and before long he was feeling truly flattered. He settled in and prepared to indulge himself, completely forgetting their dinner reservations until it was almost too late. Luckily, the restaurant was close by.

They rushed out onto Canal Street "hip to hip," as Kenyon's oil-baron daddy used to say, and strode across the way to another hotel, this one housing a French gourmet restaurant recommended by a mutual friend. They arrived to find their table ready and waiting, assisted by a folded and discreetly passed ten-dollar bill. Kenyon felt a kind of subdued excitement as he entered the room with Karen on his arm. People turned their heads, nodding as they passed by. He knew that he normally wouldn't have noticed, but somehow tonight it seemed important. He wanted to make a stir. He wanted to have fun, to get so caught up in the moment and the excitement of being with a beautiful woman that he wouldn't even think of Sabre Callot. And it seemed to be working.

Dinner couldn't have gone better. The atmosphere was pure European elegance, the service impeccable and unobtrusive. The food was, as he'd been told, superb, and that was saying something in New Orleans, where good food was considered an inalienable right. As for conversation, Karen kept up a witty, gossipy monologue, loaded with suggestive innuendo and punctuated with laughter. He just let her knock herself out, enjoying the personal attention and the obvious manner in which she bestowed it. The wine was expensive, dry and plentiful, so that they were giddy as children at a surprise party by the time they reemerged onto the street.

Kenyon hailed a hansom cab, and they sat close together in the seat while the driver guided the horse up Rue Royale to the corner of Toulouse, from which point they walked. There in the heart of the French Quarter were a number of first-class little bars. They chose one where Karen and her crowd were regulars, but there was no "crowd" that evening. They sat in a quiet corner, sipping cognac, but before long he felt boredom beginning to set in, and that spurred him to suggest they stroll over to bad, bawdy Bourbon Street.

The place was, as usual, jumping, hopping, squawking. Music and people spilled out of the buildings, off the sidewalks and galleries, and into the street itself. Pitchmen hawked every type of show imaginable, some of them truly extraordinary, in loud, strident voices. College students shrieked and howled. Hole-in-the-wall, closet-sized bars dispensed drinks to patrons lined up right on the street. Amazing numbers and types of people were doing their things. Singers sang. Strippers stripped. Dancers danced. Bands played, and magicians made magic, while vendors sold overpriced souvenirs shipped in from Korea and Japan to customers either too inebriated or exhilarated to notice or care.

They found a swinging jazz joint and pushed their way inside. The only two empty chairs in the place were all the way across a very crowded room, but the bar was on the way, so they squeezed through the haphazard mass of chairs. Karen claimed places at a table while Kenyon nabbed fresh drinks. They were sitting with a bunch of strangers, and the music was so loud they had to shout close to one another's ears in order to communicate. Kenyon was determined to make this a fun, fun evening, so he cheerfully endured. He didn't want to admit that the cure might not take, that he might already be immune to Karen's particularly lusty charm—or victim to another's.

They sat tapping their toes through the remainder of the first set, chatted during the break, and gave up conversation to listen to the first few numbers of the second set. The place was really packed now, with patrons standing three-deep along the walls and six-deep at the bar. He didn't want to brave that crush, but he was coming to rely rather heavily on alcoholic cheer to keep the evening going, and the last drinks were all gone, even the ice. He got up and made the assault, alternately elbowing through and excusing himself. He plopped down his seven bucks, got the drinks, then carefully eased himself through the mob toward the tiny table they were sharing with four new strangers. A few tense moments later, he placed the drinks in front of Karen, mission accomplished, and was preparing to take his seat. That was when he saw her.

She was edging toward the door, her back to him, her shapely hips filling a pair of tight jeans, her long, glossy hair falling over shoulders covered by a satiny, emerald green blouse. He held his breath, transfixed, unable quite to believe what he was seeing, while a little voice in the back of his head was saying, "You've had too much to drink, pal."

He told himself it wasn't her, then a man rose in her path, and she halted momentarily, tossed her dark head, and edged around him. He was talking to someone else and seemed hardly to notice, but that little toss of the head electrified Kenyon Ames, galvanized him, shook him right down to the core.

His mind was suddenly racing. What was she doing here? Was she looking for him? Who had told her to come to this place? Good Lord, what travesty had driven her out into the night like this? Where would she go? Do? He had to stop her, help her, *save* her.

"Sabre!"

Heads turned in his direction, Karen's among them, but he couldn't think of that now. She was almost to the door.

"Sabre!"

He lurched forward, stepping on toes, shoving chairs aside, pushing through the tangled maze of warm bodies. His hand fell against someone's cigarette. He jerked it away and kept moving. The door was within reach now, and Sabre was just beyond. He lunged through, and out onto the sidewalk. She was strolling down the street, a man he'd never seen before at her elbow. An old friend? A new one? Some distant member of the family? He jogged after her, caught up, reached out.

"Sabre, for heaven's sake . . ."

But it wasn't Sabre. A complete stranger blinked up at him, her face unrecognizable. She was too tall, with gray eyes and hair that now looked paler and brighter in the streetlight than it had in the dark, smoky club. He snatched his hand away, as if she, too, had burned him. He didn't know whether to be relieved or disappointed or simply embarrassed. The man said something to him, but he didn't get it and didn't care. He stammered an apology, explaining the mistake, and the pair exchanged glances that clearly said they'd smelled the alcohol on his breath. He apologized again and let them go on their way, shocked at the strength of his reaction to a woman who hadn't even been there.

What was wrong with him? Why couldn't he get that woman out of his mind? What had she done to him? In a week's time she'd turned his world upside-down, and it just didn't make any sense. There was no reason for it, no suitable explanation.

"Ames, you're insane," he muttered.

"Obviously," another voice agreed with him.

He turned to find Karen standing there, with one hip thrown out and the sequined jacket hanging from one shoulder. Her expression, disdainful at first, slowly changed to one of sympathy. She let out a long sigh and reached out a long-nailed hand to him.

"All right, chum," she said, "let's have a little talk, shall we?"

He told her everything, prattling like a schoolboy at confession after a particularly eventful month. He explained Van Garrick's unusual case, his dislike of Darryl, the decision to find the Callots. He even described the little shanty on the bayou and how Sabre had shown him her books. He told her about the rum Lennox poured into his coffee and why and how Sabre peddled her used wares. He described Ami Goula and his disturbing daughter and the special music they made there in the bayou. And he confessed to an impulsive kiss and a growing concern that had made him argue, literally argue, that she ought to come to New Orleans and Garrick House.

He went on to describe that awful dress and the insult that had been her first words of greeting. She was too innocent to know what a pathetic picture she made, too limited by her beginnings to grasp the demands of life in a place like Garrick House. Already she was suffering, and he couldn't believe now that he had just left her there to deal with that bunch alone. She was a lovely, intelligent young woman, but she simply didn't have the background to compete in the atmosphere of a place like Garrick House, and what was he going to do about it? What could he do?

He finished his tale and sighed heavily, expecting understanding, commiseration, sympathy. Karen pushed her coffee cup aside and folded her slender arms against the tabletop.

"Counselor," she said, "you're a snob."

Kenyon gaped at her, his own cup in his hands. "What are you talking about?" Karen lifted a finger to her mouth, reminding him they were not alone. Guiltily, he brought his cup down and glanced around the little café, but there were few patrons this hour of the night, and the single employee was obviously immune to shock. He didn't even appear to know they were there. Kenyon turned back to his "date" with a frown. "Are we having the same conversation here?" he asked pointedly. "I've spent the better part of the last hour explaining this mess to you and how responsible I feel, and you come up with an off-the-wall conclusion like that!" He shook his head. "Women!"

"*Woman* would be more accurate," Karen said. "This little bayou waif has really gotten under your skin, hasn't she?"

He made a shrug. "I feel responsible, if that's what you mean."

She lifted an eyebrow and pursed her mouth. "Oh, come on, Ken. She stands to inherit a fortune!"

"Not if cousin Darryl has his way!" he insisted. "Don't you get it? She's defenseless. I plucked her out of isolated poverty and plunked her down in the lap of luxury, without so much as a moment's preparation, and it is not, believe me, a benign environment. There are people in that house who want to see her out on the street! Now how is she supposed to cope in a situation like that? She might as well be on Mars!''

''So you've just got to hang around and protect her,'' Karen commented meaningfully. ''All right, the excuse will fly—a bit. So what's your problem?''

He stared at her, his mouth open for reply. The words, however, eluded him. Finally he managed a scowl. ''It's a damned nuisance, that's all!'' She laughed at him.

''You want to sleep with her.''

Trust Karen to reduce everything to its meanest terms. He rolled his eyes. ''You don't understand, at all.''

''Yes, I do.''

''She's not my type!''

''Precisely my point. She's not your type, your sort, and is therefore beneath consideration, but that doesn't keep you from being attracted to her. It just makes you ashamed that you are.''

He gaped at her. ''I haven't done anything to be ashamed of!''

''But you're afraid that you will.''

''Oh, for pity's sake, Karen, I'm not some boy with more hormones than sense.''

''Aren't you? Then why all the angst?''

''I just don't want to hurt her, that's all. She's decent, a real innocent. I don't want to give her the wrong idea.''

''In other words, you're attracted to her, but you don't want her to think you're attracted to her because she's just not suitable.''

He was getting angry. ''Holy cow, Karen, you make it sound like I look for pedigrees or something. All I'm saying is that it wouldn't be fair. She's not the kind of woman you play around with. She was raised in the middle of a swamp, miles from the nearest town. As far as I can tell, the only man she knows is that great baboon Goula. What a creep that one is.'' He shuddered for effect.

"Sounds like you rescued her from a fate worse than death to me."

"But is she any better off?" he demanded. "That's the problem."

"And it's up to little old you to see that she is, right?"

"Who else has she got?"

"Maybe no one," Karen said, "but she's sure got you, and you don't even know it yet."

"You just don't want to get it, do you?" he accused.

Karen smiled a thin, humorless smile. "All right, have it your way. But just how do you think you're going to manage this? From what you've told me, she's the emotional sort, all alone in a big house in a big city with at least two people who'd cheerfully cut her throat to get her out of the way, and you're her guardian angel, her savior, her knight in shining armor. Do you imagine she's not going to fall in love with you?"

"Not necessarily," he countered. "I'll just have to see that she doesn't."

Karen threw up her hands. "I give up. I mean, you're obviously going to ride to the rescue, and nothing I can say is going to stop you. Just remember this. If you're not very, very careful, there could be a lot of broken hearts lying around, and one of them just might be yours. Think about that, will you?"

He gave her a disdainful look and picked up his cup in a gesture of dismissal, but when he looked into it, all he saw were the black, cold dregs. He put it away, glanced at Karen's honest face, haloed by too much purchased hair and glitter, and felt a great weariness settle over him.

"I'll take you home," he said, "and I'll think about it, all right?"

She shrugged her shoulders and got to her feet. "Whatever you say. Just remember you were warned."

*   *   *

Sabre folded her hands in her lap and sat up very straight, trying hard to keep her excitement under control and earn Mallory's approval. She had been forbidden to receive her guest while wearing jeans, and had hastily changed into a peasant dress that had once belonged to her mother. The original hot pink had faded over the years to a vibrant shade of dark rose, and the crinkled, gauzy fabric had deteriorated to a soft, delicate state that made it cling to her body as she moved. The voluminous skirt reached almost to her ankles, and the full sleeves, gathered at the wrist, were overlong and had to be pushed up, making them very full, indeed. The squarish neckline called attention to her ample breasts, and the tight lacing in the midriff, played up the narrowness of her waist. Her auburn hair fell in thick, lustrous waves about her shoulders and she wore flat, dainty sandals just a size too large.

She crossed her legs at the ankles, self-conscious about the shoes, and hoped he wouldn't notice that her hands trembled amid the folds of her skirt. She still couldn't believe that he had come, but there he sat in the Sheraton armchair, nodding so intently while Aunt Mallory prattled on about the inconveniences of living in the Vieux Carré, as if *she* were the one taking up residence there.

Theo came in with the coffee service and placed it carefully on the hinged top of the piecrust table. Sabre had never before heard of a piecrust table, but Aunt Mallory was especially taken with it and often spoke of the rare curly maple of which it was constructed. Like most of the furniture in Garrick House, it was older than Methuselah, and Mallory had forbidden her to touch it. Theo had joked that he wished she'd forbid *him* to touch the "good" furniture, saying he'd smelled like beeswax and lemon oil all his adult life. To Sabre, he smelled like freshly baked bread and stewing red beans, all yeasty and mealy, the very aroma of comfort and warmth. Today, however, the whole world smelled like strong, black, chicory coffee with a touch of fondant, the latter the result of a plate of tiny cakes wrapped in pastel shades of glossy icing.

Aunt Mallory shut up long enough to pour the coffee. She asked Kenyon how he'd take his, and passed it to him black as pitch, without so much as a sniff. In her opinion, ladies didn't take their cups as strong as men, and so she tipped an alarming portion of thick cream into Sabre's without so much as raising an eyebrow in her direction. Mentally sighing, Sabre resigned herself to a tepid cup.

"This is a lovely surprise," she said, taking advantage of her aunt's preoccupation with the coffee. Mallory took time to telegraph a quelling glance as she passed the cup, but Sabre went on undaunted. "I wasn't sure I'd ever see you again."

The silver pot was set down with a clunk, and Mallory rolled her eyes heavenward. "You'll have to forgive her, Mr. Ames," she said with a sigh. "The girl has no sense of decorum. I don't know how we shall ever present her to society."

Sabre felt the hot flush of embarrassment spread over her cheeks. What had she done wrong this time? Mortified, she carefully grasped the rim of the saucer and brought it to her lap. Remembering not to lower herself to meet it, she then brought the cup up to her lips and sipped the pale brown liquid before lowering the delicate cup once more to the saucer. She felt a small pride in conducting the exercise without spilling so much as a drop, though only God knew how many countless cups of coffee she'd managed to drink without drowning herself in years past, but she knew Mallory wasn't going to notice. Kenyon seemed to, though. He winked at her from over the rim of his own cup.

"Actually, Miss Garrick," he said, "I find Sabre's frankness rather refreshing."

"You might," she came back swiftly, "but I can assure you few others will. New Orleans society clings to old and reverent ways, Mr. Ames, and my niece's education in such matters has been left sorely lacking."

Sabre did a slow burn, but said nothing. She had already learned that she couldn't defend herself against Aunt Mallory's vituperative tongue; such action would merely have her branded as recalcitrant and stubborn. It was difficult to sit meekly and accept criticism, but Sabre was bright enough to realize that what Aunt Mallory found objectionable, her contemporaries would also, and she understood that if she was to become acceptable to her grandfather, she must be acceptable to Aunt Mallory and her friends. She didn't have to like it; she just had to do it—for Butler and for Papá and for the future. Meanwhile, there was Kenyon, dear Kenyon, to lift her spirits. She admired the way he remained so cool and unruffled against all provocation, and the look he gave her now seemed to say that he admired her poise under fire. She lifted her chin, and he smiled at her.

"You have to realize, Miss Mallory, that Sabre has had no opportunity to learn the ways of New Orleans society. I have no doubt, however, that she will make an apt student."

Sabre smiled in gratitude for his eloquent defense, but she was keenly aware of her aunt's frowning scrutiny and so lifted her cup to give her mouth something else to do. Mallory made an elegant gesture of leaning back against the settee she shared with her grand-niece. At nearly seventy she was as hale and hearty as a female twenty years her junior and, Sabre had found, oddly vain for a woman who professed never to have pursued either love or marriage. Mallory surveyed both of the young people occupying her drawing room, then folded her bejeweled hands on the skirt of her prim ivory suit.

"I'm sure you're correct, Mr. Ames," she said evenly. "Unfortunately, I find I haven't the energy to instruct her.

My brother's care requires a great deal of my time and strength. We're very close, Van and I, and I wouldn't dream of abandoning him to some ill-trained nurse. Then, of course, I run the house. Someone has to. Poor Van simply cannot manage alone. It's quite a problem.'' She sighed, and brushed imaginary lint from her knee.

Sabre bit her lips, torn between hurt and blind, stubborn hope. Bravely, she put aside the hurt. "You know, Aunt Mallory," she said carefully, "I could help, really I could. I took care of Papá after he broke his back, and I learned to clean and to cook and..."

The look of sheer horror on her great-aunt's face was enough to send hope crashing. Mallory seemed offended. She primped her too-dark hair with one hand and composed her expression, as if overlooking the rankest gaffe in social grace.

"Really, my dear, I hardly think you're qualified." Sabre could have died, not simply because of the rebuff but because she'd opened herself to it. She swallowed a hot, sticky lump in her throat and stole a timid glance at Kenyon. He looked like a man who'd blundered into the wrong room, but he gave her a limp, sympathetic smile. Mallory sat up and briskly stirred her milky coffee. "I suggest we change the subject to more congenial matters," she intoned briskly. "I understand that we have mutual friends, Mr. Ames. Margo Pantier tells me they are expecting you for dinner on Thursday of next week."

Kenyon cleared his throat. "Yes. Alfred Pantier was a college mate of mine. We pledged the same fraternity at Rollins and went on to Georgetown together. His mother has graciously offered to host a little soiree in my honor."

"Well, you're in good company there," Mallory assured him. "The Pantiers are an old and respected family, and Margo herself is a Destrian."

"Yes, I understand there is some connection to the Bonaparte family."

"Oh, absolutely. You've seen the portrait of the emperor, I expect?"

Kenyon laughed. "Would Margo let anyone miss it?"

Mallory laughed, too. "Well, who could blame her? Imagine having an emperor in the family, and a French emperor, at that."

Sabre found it both odd and unreasonable that her own French forebears were looked upon with disdain but then there was no nobility in the Callot line, and to Mallory that made all the difference. She went on to name other families whose revered relatives rated mention, and there were veiled allusions to grandeur in the Garrick tree.

"But," said Mallory, "it's gauche to brag, even if Margo does do it."

Sabre wanted to roll her eyes. The elitism, the pure snobbery that was part of such talk, made her ill. What difference did it make who Margo Whatever's ancestors were? She left her cup and saucer balanced on her knee and folded her arms across her middle, steeling herself against reaction.

"Sabre," Mallory chided, interrupting her ancestor-fawning long enough to scold, "I will not allow you to spill the contents of that cup on a genuine Hansen rug. If you've no interest in drinking your *café au lait*, be good enough to give it back so I can put it safely away. Of course, it's not the polite thing to do, but it's better than coffee stains on an expensive carpet."

"Yes, Aunt Mallory," Sabre muttered through her teeth, stiffly handing over the cup. A bit of the light brown liquid sloshed over into the saucer. She was in no mood to apologize, but she made herself explain, "It's just that I prefer *café noir*."

Mallory placed the cup and saucer on the tray and made a show of wiping her hands on a crisp, melon pink napkin. "Far be it from me to criticize," she began, doing just that, "but in my day, young women were too delicate to take their coffee black." She let her hands fall heavily to her lap and addressed her guest. "So like her mother. I never understood this hostility to convention."

Sabre thought she would explode. She gulped air, straining for composure, but she just couldn't remain silent. It was one thing to accept unfair criticism of one's self, but quite another to allow criticism of someone dear.

"My mother was a very conventional woman," she protested, struggling to keep her tone even, but Mallory ignored her.

"I tried so hard with Gamelin," she went on. "Van was a man in his prime, then, but he was so very active in business and the community, and though outwardly Gamelin was a docile child, she could never be counted upon to do the proper thing."

It was too much. Sabre wanted to be calm, but honor forbade sitting idle while this harridan maligned her dear mother's memory.

"That is not true!" she insisted, her tone rising despite one more desperate attempt to retain her composure. "My mother always did the proper thing," she went on. Mallory huffed and shook her head sadly, as if witnessing a particularly pathetic delusion. Sabre was gasping, shaking. "Just because she fell in love with a man outside her social circle—"

"There, you see," Mallory interrupted, addressing herself to Kenyon. "Not what I would call reasonable behavior." Kenyon had a pained expression on his face.

"Highly emotional, to be sure," he began, and Sabre's mouth fell open, "but understandable when you consider the natural inclination to defend one's parent."

Emotional? Understandable? What condescension! Sabre felt wounded, betrayed. It was really the last straw. She came to her feet and threw up her hands.

"*De pis en pis!*" she exclaimed, no longer caring to be reasonable.

"Well, really," Mallory sniffed, folding her hands, but Kenyon merely blinked.

"I beg your pardon?"

"From worse to worse!" she declared. "Her, I understand, but I thought you were my friend!"

Now *his* mouth fell open. "I was trying to defend you!"

"If that's your defense, I shudder at your condemnation!"

"Now you really are being unreasonable," he said flatly, setting aside his cup.

"It's impossible!" Mallory wailed. "She's sullen and intractable, with manners like a peasant! God knows I've tried, but it's useless, utterly useless!"

Sabre whirled on her, realizing that once again she had fallen into Mallory's trap. Once again she had disgraced herself. It was utterly useless, she saw. Suddenly, she wanted desperately to go home, to tip rum into her father's cup and peddle her worn books for nickels and dimes. She wanted to see Butler and hear the music of his accordion. Even Ami Goula seemed benign and comforting, at the moment. She felt her chin begin to tremble, and to her mortification she realized she was once again at the point of tears. But not this time. This time, it was too much. Defiantly, she turned her back on Mallory—and encountered the troubled countenance of Kenyon Ames. The misery on his face stunned and confused her. No longer did she see anger or defensiveness, just pure, abject misery. She blinked back the tears, clenched her jaws firmly, and lifted her chin, unconsciously ruffling the hair upon her shoulders.

Something very strange happened, then. A look almost of shock came over him, followed quickly by a deliberate, even confident, determination. He got up and gave his head a little jerk, squaring his shoulders.

"If you'll permit me," he said, bowing slightly toward Mallory. Sabre never knew whether the liberty was given or taken, for Mallory's reaction simply didn't register, or if it did his next words knocked it right out of her head. "Sabre," he said, "I want you to come and stay with me."

Chapter Seven

There were twin gasps, but neither Mallory nor Sabre recognized the irony in their agreement.

"Mister Ames!" Mallory scolded, but Sabre was quite incapable of speech.

"It's a reasonable solution," Kenyon insisted, his attention centering on the older of the two women. "I can't help feeling responsible, having brought Sabre here myself, and since she is obviously a burden—" Sabre squeaked a protest, but as it was incomprehensible, it went ignored "—I feel it would be better for everyone, if she stayed with me. Mr. Garrick obviously wishes to become well-acquainted with his granddaughter, but as her presence in the house distresses you, it seems to me a compromise is in order. If Sabre stayed elsewhere and simply came to visit at times convenient to you . . ."

Mallory suddenly stood, her back board straight. "I'm afraid what you propose is most improper," she insisted.

"It needn't be," he came back smoothly. "I'll see to it she's well chaperoned. If necessary, we can find alternative lodgings. The important thing is that she be available to Mr. Garrick and that she receive proper instruction, which I feel qualified to give her."

Sabre's eyebrows rose in tandem. *Instruction?* Was she a *child* who required *instruction*? She could see that Aunt Mallory thought so; she was actually considering this insanity! But surely it wasn't possible. How could she share a house with Kenyon Ames—unless... She thought of that kiss in the dappled shade of the bayou, of the look on his face there on the embankment at Piroux's when she'd stood near him and wondered if he might kiss her again. She thought of his skillful defenses, the comfort of his strong arms, the encouragement in the clasp of his hand. Was it possible...? Might he actually...? Or was it simply, as he said, that he felt responsible? She didn't know what to think, but she did know how she felt about Kenyon Ames at this point, and it wouldn't do for her to put herself too much in the way of temptation, especially if he was as attracted to her as she was to him.

"I can't," she said, finding her voice at last. Kenyon shot her a surprised look, but Mallory paid no attention.

"It's Van's decision," she said, as if Sabre had never spoken. "I'll speak to him." Mallory turned on her heel and walked out of the room.

Sabre's heart was beating like a trip-hammer. She stared at Kenyon, who twisted his mouth into a comical smile and shrugged.

"This isn't happening," she said, astounded.

"You're right. It isn't."

She blinked at him. "What?"

"You said, 'This isn't happening,' and I said, 'You're right. It isn't.'"

She put both hands to her head, completely muddled, especially as he was smiling in the most irritatingly self-satisfied fashion.

"I don't know what's going on," she said, "but I won't—"

"No, no, of course not," he agreed hastily.

"The very idea is crazy!"

"Possibly," he said. "However, you must realize that you're at something of a disadvantage here. Your cousin has the gift of the chameleon. He changes his colors to fit his surroundings. You, on the other hand, don't have a single bit of artifice at your disposal, and with Mallory constantly cutting you to ribbons and keeping you in an emotional state, you can't possibly adjust. But now tell me, Sabre, if you or I were to go to Van Garrick and say, well, that Mallory was being unfair, for example, what do you suppose his reaction would be?"

That was easy. She'd seen enough of Van and Mallory's relationship, and remembered enough of her mother's stories, to know what the answer would be.

"He wouldn't believe it, and I'd be labeled as troublesome."

"And Darryl would quite clearly have the upper hand," he pointed out. "On the other hand, if Mallory herself should go to her brother and plead for release from some of her responsibilities . . ."

"He'd listen." She was beginning to see a pattern here. "But you know she's going to blame me. That woman hates me, Kenyon. *Mon Dieu!* You should hear some of the things she says to me, always disguised as instruction, of course, but—" It suddenly became clear. She stared at him, and a slow smile stretched his mouth into a perfect crescent revealing white, even teeth.

"She can't afford to tip her hand, can she? She'll say she's tried to instruct you, but that she just doesn't have the energy to cope. She'll deny any bias, of course, but she's going to argue in favor of allowing me to take over for her because she really doesn't like you any more than she liked your mother or your mother's mother or any other woman her brother has ever cared for. It's common knowledge, Sabre, with everyone who knows them except Van himself, and she's going to do everything in her power to protect her position, you see?''

She did see, quite clearly. "But propriety is quite important to Grandfather, and he wouldn't allow a single man to move me into his house, no matter how innocent it was.''

"True. But I'm not just any single man, Sabre. I'm part of the right crowd. It wouldn't be proper for me to take you into my residence, but who better, may I ask, to take the strain off dear Mallory?''

She was speechless. To be removed from beneath Aunt Mallory's thumb, to be "tutored" by Kenyon. It wasn't perfect, of course. Mallory couldn't help but dig at her every now and again. Still, with Kenyon's help, anything seemed possible—anything, at all. She didn't know what to say, what to do. It was just all so incredible. It was Kenyon, wonderful, wonderful Kenyon, and it never occurred to her not to act on that knowledge. The people she knew, vibrant, earthy, demonstrative, were given to extravagant expressions of emotion, and she simply followed a well-established pattern. Throwing her arms wide, she launched herself at him.

"You're wonderful!" She hit him in what was almost a tackle, arms flying about him. He stumbled backward and caught her against him.

"Whoa!''

"It's brilliant! Genius!''

He was laughing and trying to keep his feet under him, while she was going up and down, toe to heel, toe to heel, and hugging him in frenetic excitement.

"*Remercier vous très beaucoup,* Kenyon! *Remercier vous très beaucoup!*"

"Yes, yes. Great! You're happy. Great! Don't break my neck!"

Her arms flew up. Her breath came in a shrill gasp. She didn't want to hurt him. She wanted to hug him! And she did. Again. Going up on tiptoe, she threw her arms about his neck and squeezed. And then it all changed. Suddenly it was only her own laughter she heard, and she wasn't hopping up and down, either, merely moving against him because his arms were locked in the small of her back, holding her against him. She froze, the air stopping in her lungs, heart lurching. Slowly, she tilted her head back, staring into eyes the color of an evening sky after the sun has pulled its last orange ray below the horizon. What she saw there caused her to melt against him, lift upward, and bring her mouth to his.

He said something, one word, one syllable, a sound. It didn't matter what. It was the expression of surrender, of capitulation to one's own desire, and with it his mouth seized hers in a kiss that reached deeply into the soft well of her being.

"*He kissed me, and I was lost.*" The words rang round inside her head. It was her mother's voice she heard, explaining, in that dreamy way of hers, how it had been with them, and for the first time Sabre really understood. For the first time, Sabre was lost, completely, happily, delightedly lost.

She felt certain she'd have melted and run down to the floor in a puddle at his feet, but his arms were there to press her against him, his mouth to hold her, his hands to knead and mold and fit her pliant shape to his. At any rate, she wasn't about to let go of him. Her arms were curled about his neck, her fingers splayed between his shoulder blades and moving quite of their own accord through the silky hair at the back of his head. Her mouth was a willing captive, seeking only to conform in path and pose to his, constantly opening itself to him, while other parts of her body responded accordingly, parts she couldn't quite identify, shifting and growing as if to make space for him.

She was concentrating on that phenomenon, on the sensations changing and thrilling her body, when his hands went suddenly to her face. In another moment, she realized his mouth was detaching itself from hers, and in the next she was swaying, her arms empty, the sturdy wall of his body no longer pressed to hers. She couldn't move, couldn't think, and then her ears picked up on the clack-clack-clack echoing in the entry and identified it. Someone was walking across the marble floor of the entry, down to the main hall.

"Mallory," Kenyon whispered, his very tone a plea. Sabre gasped, whirled and clasped her hands together, just before Mallory appeared in the doorway. Mallory looked at them, standing side by side, and a frown creased her pale face. It was disapproval, quick and flat, but in it there was no apparent recognition of what had passed between them only a moment before.

"Van wants to see you," she said tersely. "Both of you."

It was neither the worst interview imaginable nor the best. As Kenyon had predicted, her grandfather flatly refused to allow her to live with anyone other than himself. Motive was never discussed—not his, not Kenyon's. Propriety was what counted, or rather, the appearance of propriety. But there was Mallory's complaint to consider, and a sour, frowning Mallory to give the complaint weight, however gently she'd managed to phrase it initially. With just a word or two of suggestion, Kenyon managed to plant the idea that Sabre ought to receive instruction and that he ought to be the one to give it. After that, it was merely a matter of allowing Van to manipulate him into agreeing to "sponsor" her.

Financial arrangements were discussed, as it was agreed by all—except Sabre, of course—that a suitable wardrobe was desperately needed. Kenyon was to front the money, which Sabre was to repay, with interest, as a condition of her inheritance, were she to receive one. Should the inheritance go to Darryl, Kenyon would simply lose his "investment," a condition to which he agreed without a moment's hesitation.

Sabre was flabbergasted by the whole thing and not at all certain she ought to be agreeing, but as it wasn't left to her, she really didn't have any choice except to go along. Not that she would have done anything else given the prospect of spending several hours a day in the "instructive" company of Kenyon Ames.

It actually turned out to be less charming than she'd expected. They worked out a schedule. Four afternoons a week were given over to instruction. Kenyon explained that the other days were for his "social obligations," for friends who expected to enjoy his company and, too often, his expertise. Sabre would have liked to see him daily, even to be invited along on some of those obligatory social occasions, but she did not complain. How could she? He had moved into an apartment in the Vieux Carré and put his home life and most of his business on hold in order to rescue her. That was literally what he had done, rescued her from the most lethal applications of Mallory's tongue. That didn't mean she had escaped Mallory altogether, far from it, in fact, but with Theo to keep her spirits up during the difficult times, her books to escape to during the worst of them and Kenyon to look forward to most afternoons, she felt fortunate, indeed.

Kenyon was not, however, the indulgent schoolmaster she'd expected. He was kind and pleasant, but terribly serious, and he was intent upon teaching her the most seemingly useless things, like the difference between a regular fork and all the other kinds: salad, desert, oyster.... And then there were spoons and knives and a ridiculous variety of serving utensils and glasses and plates and on and on. Why anyone wanted to so complicate such a simple matter as eating was quite beyond her, and they experienced some sharp words over her continually repeating the sentiment.

From dining, they moved on to invitations: wording them, sending them, receiving them, replying to them. Next came standards of address: Mr., Mrs., Miss, Ms., and all manner of legal and military titles. He made up names and assigned titles to them and tested her memory of them. She was irreverent and exuberant and determined to have a bit of fun in the process. He laughed, despite himself, recovered, remonstrated and began again, sterner.

She worked hard for him, but the whole thing seemed so silly so often that she just couldn't maintain decorum. After a bit, she would get playful and he would get tickled, and they'd be laughing instead of working. Then he'd get mad and solemn and read her off, and she'd start apologizing.

"Yes, I realize how important this is. I know how hard you're working to help me. I understand that you feel responsible, but... Of course, I'll cooperate. No, really. I'm sorry. It won't happen again, I promise."

But, of course, it would, and sometimes he'd leave mad, and sometimes she'd lean over and lightly kiss his cheek, and he'd clear his throat and make a quick, rather desperate departure. But not once, ever, did he kiss her, and she began to feel confused and bereft and lost, so that finally after a couple of weeks she didn't tease anymore, and it became his turn to lighten the mood. He did it by announcing that they were going shopping.

Just the idea of a day out was enough to make Sabre tingle with excitement, and a day of shopping, despite her misgivings, was enough to make her positively giddy. Never, in her life, had she actually been shopping for anything other than the genuine necessities: grocery staples, fishing line, kerosene, a very few school supplies. The only articles of clothing she had ever purchased had been for others: a T-shirt with a pocket for Butler's birthday, a lacy hankie for Mother's Day, white socks for Papá for Christmas. The idea of buying things for herself was foreign and a little frightening, and she felt strongly that the money Kenyon was spending on her was a loan which she must repay at some future date.

She'd tried to imagine what she would buy, maybe a pretty dress for Sunday mass or a long-sleeved blouse of fine cotton with embroidery on the collar and cuffs. If she bought the blouse, she could wear it with jeans and skirts, and it could then do double duty. She decided to prolong the decision and thereby the pleasure in making it.

Actually, she didn't see what was wrong with the wardrobe her mother had left behind. What if the garments themselves were twenty years old? They were in good condition, almost like new, and of obvious quality. Most of them were a serviceable fit, though her mother had been a tiny thing in her youth, with a surprisingly flat bosom. Theo had laughingly told her that flat bosoms had been in style, but she couldn't imagine such a thing. Everyone knew round, full bosoms were one of a woman's best assets. Anyway, she had told Aunt Mallory that, given enough time, needles and thread, she could satisfactorily alter many of the items in her mother's wardrobe to suit herself, but Mallory had only rolled her eyes and said, "Why me?"

To prove the point, Sabre had spent the evening slimming down the legs and adjusting the hems of a pair of white pants. They rode rather low on the hips, which was inconvenient, but she solved that problem by wearing a long, loose, gauzy blouse belted with a scarf. She had no option but to wear sandals, for it seemed her mother had worn little else, and they were the most satisfactory fit. For the big day, she chose neat little tan ones with laces that crisscrossed and buckled around the ankles. She opted for simplicity with her hair, brushing it until it gleamed, then parting it and tucking one side behind her ear. She considered rolling up the sides the way she had that first day in New Orleans when Kenyon had complimented her, but she decided to save that for a special occasion, trusting that there would be a special occasion. The look Kenyon gave her when she joined him in the private salon, a small but exquisitely furnished room beneath the staircase, told her she had chosen wisely, and they went out together on what seemed a great adventure to Sabre.

The first shop proved to be a disappointment, however. Everything was shiny and new and luxurious, but the clothing was much too frivolous for Sabre's liking and, she insisted, much too expensive. Beads and sequins and feathers were simply not her style, and she frankly couldn't imagine anyone whose style they might be, especially not at the prices she heard quoted. Kenyon gave her no argument when she asked to leave, and after some discussion they wound up at an upscale shopping center near the Superdome. Sabre was overwhelmed. She'd never seen so many gleaming surfaces in one place or so many well-dressed people, not to mention so many clothes!

There were several different departments devoted to dresses of one sort or another and others dealing exclusively with undergarments and shoes and nightgowns and... Well, the list was exhaustive, as Sabre soon discovered. She hardly knew where to begin, but Kenyon solved that problem by asking for a "personal shopper," someone who could judge the situation and make the appropriate suggestions.

Sabre had never had such fun. She tried on everything an entire team of clerks presented her. It was a veritable orgy of discovering and fitting and laughing and whirling in front of mirrors. At some point, she realized Kenyon was enjoying himself, too, critiquing the various outfits she modeled for him and just watching the transformations. Most of it was just fun, she realized. After all, when was *she* ever going to need a ball gown or a silk suit or hand-painted shawls? There were a few small, frivolous items she just couldn't resist, though, such as a cute little garter belt and colored stockings with dainty butterflies embroidered on the ankles and a peach-colored bra made mostly of lace and wire. Those items were the beginning and the end of what she considered splurging, however, and she was appalled when Kenyon and the clerk began to insist that she was going to need a whole array of undergarments to wear with the dozen or so outfits upon which they'd decided.

Sabre could not believe they expected her to buy all those things. Moreover, she couldn't accept that two or three garments were not sufficient for her needs. Kenyon argued that different types of garments were suitable for different types of occasions and that she could very well find herself in need of several changes in the space of a single day. The idea seemed ludicrous to Sabre, and the discussion eventually became quite heated, with Kenyon insisting that his opinion prevail. Sabre felt sure that he was overstating the need, but when the saleslady informed her that any unworn item could be returned for full refund, she gave in.

That put a stop to the shouting, but not the argument, which they continued over lunch—gumbo and cheese sandwiches eaten in a quaint little sidewalk café in the Vieux Carré. Afterward, they carried the "discussion" onto the street, where Sabre was so busy arguing that people shouldn't look down their noses at other people just because they wore the same dress once too often that she failed to notice the direction in which they were walking until Kenyon stopped, took out a set of keys, and inserted one into the lock of a narrow cast-iron gate. Momentarily stalled, Sabre took a moment to look around her. The sense of direction and place developed by the need to survive without street signs and clear-cut lanes served her well, even in the heart of the city. The placement of the sun in the sky told her the street faced west—more or less—which meant the street ran north and south. The gate was on their right, hence, they had been walking north, away from the shopping center and, she felt certain, the street trolley. But why? Despite the intensity of her feelings on the subject of money spent on her behalf, she phrased the question delicately.

"Um, where exactly are we?"

The gate swung open, creaking slightly on its painted metal hinges. He struck a defensive pose. "I want to make a point," he said, "and the best way to do that seems to be by example."

"All right. But that doesn't answer the question, does it?"

He took a deep breath, nostrils flaring slightly, and slowly exhaled. "We're at the apartment of a good friend of mine."

"Oh," she said, secretly pleased. "I'd like to meet your friend."

"Ah." He scratched his ear with the tip of the key in his hand. "Well, that's a problem. He's not around at the moment. In fact, he's not on the continent at the moment."

Sabre blinked. "Then why have we come to see him?"

"We haven't," he told her. "We've come to see me, or rather, my clothes."

Sabre folded her arms. "That's the most ridiculous thing I've ever heard!"

He smiled and nodded. "So it is. Nevertheless, I insist."

"And if I refuse?" she retorted.

He showed her his neat, white teeth. "I've had enough argument, Sabre. I'm trying to make a point."

"I don't think I'm interested," she told him petulantly, at which point he ground those neat, white teeth.

"All right," he said tersely. "Suit yourself." He walked through the gate and began to climb the wrought-iron stairs wedged into the four-foot space between buildings. "When you get tired of standing on the sidewalk, come on up. It's the second door on the landing," he called down to her.

Sabre would have thrown a rock at him, if there'd been one at hand. As it was, she either had to stand there on the sidewalk, take herself home—and she could—or go on up. She watched him disappear around the corner at the top of the stairs, then looked down the street in the direction from which they'd come. All right. She could get home. No problem. The trolley left from the corner of Canal and Bourbon, which ran roughly east to west. Or did it? She looked up at the sky one more time and this time found the sun hanging over a three-story building on the *north*west corner? She bit her lip. All right, so the streets weren't laid out on a true lateral. She could still find her way home if she wanted to—which she didn't, really.

She walked through the gate, pulled it closed and started up the stairs. Well, why shouldn't she go up? She owed him her attention, at least. So what if they were going to be alone up there? They were adults, after all. This wasn't the Middle Ages. She was a grown woman on her own in a big city. All right, not entirely on her own, but that was the point, wasn't it? However pigheaded, Kenyon was her mentor, her friend. And if that was all there was to it, why was her heart beating like a big brass drum? She reached the top of the stairs and paused for breath, telling herself she ought to go right back down again. Then she turned right and walked along the landing.

The second door was standing open, and she made up her mind to go in without really making it up, at all, only to find that he wasn't even in the room. It was a charming room, all plants and wicker furniture and cushions in bright, vibrant colors that made her feel as if she'd just stepped onto a tropical island. The high, sky blue ceiling gave the room an open feeling, and the carpet was the color of sand on a beach. Lights were tucked cleverly in the small jungle of potted plants, so lamps were unnecessary. The casual inclusion of a hammock among the furniture and the use of a thick beach towel as an area rug added to the aura. She could almost feel the breeze off the ocean, except that it was a breeze through the large French window overlooking the courtyard. All in all, it was a room where a woman could sit back, put her feet up and enjoy a juicy book between naps, and it didn't do a thing to put Sabre at ease.

A wall of hand-turned spindles wrapped in ivy growing from a kind of long, narrow box sunk into the floor divided the living area from the dining area, which Sabre was surprised to see was the larger and completely taken up with an odd, horseshoe-shaped, glass-topped table that could accommodate—she counted mismatched wicker chairs— eighteen! At the end of the divider, which was shorter than the room was narrow, was a doorway that opened into a narrow hall, and it was there where Kenyon reappeared.

"Well, come on," he said, as if he'd never had a doubt she would be standing there, then promptly disappeared again. Sabre glowered and walked across the room. Once in the little hallway, she could see that it ran between two bedrooms, with a bath opening off its center, an arrangement she found both convenient and sensible. Kenyon was standing in one of the bedroom doorways, a clothes hanger in his hand. "I'm just tidying up," he said, sounding rather apologetic. "Forgive the mess."

He walked away, and Sabre carefully strolled down the hallway and leaned through the doorway. The room was larger than she'd expected. Another French window opened onto the landing and the courtyard below. On one side of it stood a large, unmade bed draped in filmy mosquito netting; at its foot was an upholstered bench. Another stood against the wall to her immediate left, surrounded by plants. A towel had been left draped over it, and another lay in a damp pile on the hardwood floor. The wall opposite the window and bed contained two doors, the one in which she stood and another through which Kenyon darted to snatch up the two towels.

"Okay," he said, his hands full of towels, "you can go in now."

She gave him a blank look. "Go in where?"

"The closet," he said, lifting a towel to indicate the remaining door. She stared at him.

"Why would I want to go in there?"

"Because," he said, "that's where my clothes are." She remained confused, and he hastened to explain. "It's a kind of closet with a hall, see. It opens on the other side into the bathroom, and there are racks and shelves on each end and a few drawers—enough. Anyway, that's not all of my clothes, of course. I only brought one suitcase in the beginning, but then I had Kathy—that's my secretary, Kathryn—send out some other things. And then I had her send out a few more and a few more until most of what I actually wear is out here, now, instead of in Houston. You following?"

She just stared at him, then she figured what the heck and walked over to the closet. It was a very clever arrangement. The rods were not full but full enough, and it was the same with the shelves. She had no idea what was in the drawers and didn't intend to find out.

"Okay," she said, leaning against the doorjamb and folding her arms. "So what's this point you're struggling to make?"

He stared at her, then pushed past and carried the towels into the bathroom. "The point is," he said, coming back, 'the average person has a lot more clothes than you seem to hink he does."

She smirked. "First of all, *bon ami*, you're not what I'd all an average person, and second, you don't honestly xpect me to believe that all of these clothes are yours, do ou?"

He sighed and reached out to seize her wrist. "All right, Aiss Smarty, see for yourself."

He hauled her straight through and out the other side, cross the bath—which seemed to be all wood, glass brick, lants and white tile—and into a second closet, a perfect vin of the first, except that it contained even more clothes han the other one.

"These are Claude's." He snatched a white linen coat om the rod and held it up beneath his chin. It was enornous.

"Hardly a fit," he pointed out, and back they went the ay they'd come. Drawing her fully into the first closet, he ung the coat on the rack among several others, all of which ere obviously smaller. "Now do you believe me?" This me, *he* leaned against the doorjamb and folded his arms, hile Sabre looked around her once more.

She recognized the slacks he'd worn to call at the Garrick louse only yesterday and, on a shelf behind them, the shirt, eatly folded. There on the floor were the canvas shoes he'd orn back in the bayou, clean now and stuffed with paper. he saw a white suit that looked almost like a uniform and black one very like it but with an extra row of buttons. here were others, too, one in a small, neat kind of check id another with very thin, widely spaced stripes. In addin there were several differently colored slacks draped over added hangers and a number of jeans. On the shelves were any folded shirts, some of them solid colors, others simy patterned, in crisp cottons and soft knits. And all this presented only what the secretary had sent out. That was a pretty friendly secretary, she mused, if she didn't mind going through the boss's clothes. On the other hand, *she* was going through his clothes—and that was a very friendly thing, indeed, even *intimate.*

"You've made your point," she said, quickly exiting into the bedroom. She thought of the clothes her mother had left behind at Garrick House, realizing for the first time that, when coupled with the shabby but ample wardrobe she'd always kept at home, her mother had been very well outfitted. That being the case, she began to understand the standard to which Grandfather—and certainly Aunt Mallory— expected her to rise. She took a deep breath and felt suddenly irritated. "I just don't see why anyone would ever need that many clothes!"

It was then that Kenyon began to lecture her, suggesting places and events where she might be expected to put in an appearance as a real New Orleans Garrick, and demonstrating from his own closet what, in her place, he might wear. At first, she just couldn't believe people really did these things, let alone that she might one day do them, as well, but as the demonstration continued, she found that she was having a pretty good time. As his lecture progressed, Kenyon took to spreading completed ensembles on the bed and rearranging them, then started hanging them on various objects about the room, and finally spread them right across the floor. To her surprise, Sabre found that the white and black suits were tuxedos, the male equivalent of the ball gown, and when he put them together with pleated shirts, cummerbunds and various ties, she saw just how attractive they could be.

It was all rather intriguing, really, and while they were supposing, she got to supposing what she might wear if she were to accompany him to these various imaginary outings. When they got to the formal dinner party, she dreamed up a little black dress very similar to one Kenyon had insisted she purchase that very afternoon. It was "tea length," according to the salesperson, had a straight skirt slit up the back, "dolman" sleeves, padded shoulders and a flattering "scooped" neckline that showed just a hint of cleavage. She figured the one real strand of pearls she'd inherited from her mother would set it off perfectly, and was delighted when Kenyon agreed. He then proposed a full-fledged ball—no costumes, just dinner, dancing, champagne and rubbing elbows with the city's elite.

"Now remember," he said, "we're not just any old guests. We are *announced*. That means a table just off the dance floor, lots of people coming up to say hello and watching from the lesser seats in the balconies, waiters at our elbows."

Sabre closed her eyes and described a dress any woman in her right mind would treasure: a strapless bodice of regal green satin, a full, full skirt, ankle-length, and constructed of yards and yards of soft tulle showing large, pale roses in swirling garlands on a background of almost white with a delicate tinge of bluish green, and around the waist, a long velvet ribbon tied in a big bow that trailed down the back.

"You'll wear your hair up and caught with a diamond pin," Kenyon told her, as if she'd made the vision real for him. "And we'll hang diamonds from your ears and drape them about your neck and wrist."

"And we'll dance," she said, so caught up in the dream she could hear the music.

"And dance," he said, taking her in his arms.

"And dance!"

He whirled her about the room. Only avoiding the clothing strewn across the floor kept this dream from being real. But then she stepped squarely in the middle of a white shirt and, in trying not to soil it, slipped and would have fallen had he not caught her to him. His strong arm clasped across the small of her back so tightly that her heels left the floor, leaving only her toes and his strong arm to bear her weight. Everything stopped all at once: the music, the vision, movement, even her heart. Suddenly they were once more frozen into a moment of high-voltage contact, where all those mundane, automatic reflexes seemed nonexistent, things such as breathing, blinking, thinking, while other natural physical senses were wildly exaggerated.

The room was a veritable cauldron of colognes, none of them readily identifiable, all of them together making a light, crisp brew that seemed to enliven not only the nose but the taste buds, as well. It was a heady, fragrant wine that permeated, rather than was ingested. Simultaneously, the air took on a cool, silken feel against the skin, like a weightless, invisible cloud of chiffon gently swirling around them. At the same time, everything melted into a soft, vibrant blue. The world was blue, sparkling, jewel-like, mesmerizing, and when his hand spread against her cheek, it was as if heat radiated through her body, licking into flame where her hips met his and searing down along the remainder of her length.

She didn't know who moved first. She only knew that somehow their mouths came together, and the kiss she'd been waiting for, dreaming of, trusting to come, was finally happening and happening with such intensity that all she could do was just hang on. Her blue world canted, dropping them to their knees. She shut it out with lowered lids, leaving that vibrantly conscious part of herself to register the sensations flooding her. So much was happening at once. His hands slid over her body, warming skin that prickled and iced in their wake. She shuddered with wave after exquisite, racking wave and sought to heat herself by pressing her body into his, creating other unbearable needs to be sated and stoked with a touch, a pressure, a stroke. His tongue parted her teeth, meeting her own and challenging it, so that they jousted and tasted one another with feverish boldness. But it was simply not enough.

They went down on their sides, legs twining, hands fumbling at restraints and barriers. Then, with just the slightest encouragement from him, a mere shifting of weight, Sabre rolled onto her back, Kenyon beside her, his hand pushing beneath her blouse, searing the naked flesh from curvaceous hip to the peaked pinnacles of her breasts. And still it was not enough.

She literally pulled him atop her, her hands clutching at bunched muscle and loose fabric, legs parting to accommodate his weight. His body moved against hers in the most provocative manner, sharing the need to constantly renegotiate what seemed a perfect fit in an attempt to achieve a constantly higher perfection, until it seemed a genuine joining was the only remaining option and even that would not be enough. It was agony and heaven, all at once, need and fulfillment leading to ever greater need, until at last he broke his mouth from hers.

With his arms locked tightly about her, his quick, shallow breaths fanning the hollow where her jaw met the curve of her ear, she felt long, rocking shivers move through him. The clamorings of desire and satisfaction began to recede. A little frightened but deliriously happy, she held him until he relaxed and, shifting the bulk of his weight, pulled away a bit. His hand slid up the slender column of her throat to cup her chin, his thumb tracing the shape of her mouth, and those evening blue eyes delved into hers, then skittered away. She sought them again but this time found them troubled and wary. The first wave of warning reverberated through her, but then he smiled tenderly and his hand stroked her cheek. He placed a kiss upon her temple and another between her slender brows and a third, final one upon her lips. Then with a sigh, he rolled away from her.

"I have to put a stop to this now," he told her softly, "before I do something I'll only regret."

Chapter Eight

There's no denying a physical attraction, and God knows I feel a certain responsibility, but...oh, how do I say this?"

He paced the floor in front of her, as she sat on the edge of his bed. Sabre put a hand to her hair, smoothing it, her thoughts slow and muddled.

"You don't have to say anything, Kenyon," she told him in a small, confused voice. "I, too, am responsible, *oui*?"

"No! Not in the way I mean."

"But, Kenyon, there was no force. I wanted to make love with you."

"We didn't make love!"

"I didn't say that we did. I said I wanted to."

"Don't say that, Sabre! Just don't say such things. It isn't done. It isn't . . . right."

"What is *not* right about it, Kenyon? Is it wrong to be honest?"

"Sometimes, yes, especially when you haven't thought

things through, when you don't understand what's happening.''

"Do you think I fail to understand desire, Kenyon? Do you think just because I'm a virgin that I haven't wanted to love?''

"Oh, God," he said, sending his hand down the back of his head. "That does it. That really settles it. Sabre, listen to me." He leaned into the bed with one knee. His fingers skimmed her cheek. "You're a beautiful woman.''

That was good to hear. She smiled warmly, her original unease giving way to natural assumption.

"Thank you. I think you're beautiful, too.''

"Uh, no." He promptly withdrew to stand apart from her, his hand going to his forehead. "You misunderstand me. I was going to say that although you are a very beautiful woman—and you are, no doubt about it—you're not ... the right woman for me.''

Sabre needed a moment to let that sink in, and once it did, she didn't like the sound of it, at all. Could she have misread all those signs? Hadn't he wanted to kiss her there in the bayou? Hadn't he been thinking what she had been thinking all that morning? It had seemed so. Hadn't he argued that she belonged here in New Orleans? And hadn't he brought her himself, coaxing her like a balky child with a sweetmeat? Hadn't he been kind and supportive, making himself available to her when she'd had no reason to expect it of him? Hadn't he rescued her from Mallory's attacks with a brilliant scheme all his own? And hadn't he sponsored her, tutored her, played the patient mentor, when reason and responsibility called for him to be in another place at another matter? And hadn't he kissed her, wanted her just now? If she was not the "right" woman for him, why had he done all those things? She shook her head.

"I don't understand.''

He sighed and sat down beside her. "I know you don't, and so I'm going to explain it to you very carefully." And he did—and gently destroyed all her lovely illusions.

They were from different worlds. In the time he could give her, she couldn't hope to understand how different. It was wrong of him, he said, to kiss her when he knew it might mean something to her that it couldn't possibly mean to him. He was not used to making permanent alliances with the women in his life. His career made that impossible. Relationships were so hard to maintain, even when the two parties had a great deal in common, and his long absences and eclectic life-style added insurmountable difficulty. He understood that a temporary liaison was not the "done thing" for such a woman as herself, and should he allow himself to succumb to the natural physical attraction between them, he would only wind up feeling more responsible and guilty than when he had begun.

"I realized too late, you see, just what I had done when I urged you to leave the bayou and come here. At the time it seemed so right to remove you from, well, a difficult situation there."

Sabre sighed, a great gloom coming over her. *God save me,* she thought, *from the best intentions of a genuine gentleman.* For whatever else Kenyon Ames might be, he was that, and she was not beneath wishing he was less. She listened morosely as he counseled her to put from her mind the idea of romance and think of him as a very good friend and a teacher.

"You have an opportunity here, Sabre, far greater than any I could give you. Let me help you attain the new life you came in search of. Don't let's ruin it over what is surely a passing attraction. I promise, on my solemn honor, that what happened tonight will not happen again."

De pis en pis, she thought sadly. *From worse to worse. With no end in sight.*

* * *

Sabre brushed the egg yolk from her fingertips, then carefully wiped them on a tea towel. God forbid she should get a spot on her khaki-colored silk blouse. Why had she allowed herself to be talked into buying such a blouse, anyway? And what did Aunt Mallory have against jeans? She'd been told in no uncertain terms to change out of them the instant she stopped her "piddling" in the kitchen. As if that wasn't bad enough, the cookies she and Mary Jill were painting looked like soggy, surrealistic lumps. She must have done something wrong, but now what could she do about it? *De pis en pis.* Always, it seemed, from worse to worse. But who noticed besides her? No one. And she intended for it to stay that way.

As far as Kenyon and Grandfather and Theo and even Mallory were concerned, she had achieved amazing progress, from peasant to aristocrat. And wasn't it what she had wanted? Why then did she feel so unhappy? But what did it matter? Butler still had his chance as long as she didn't blow the inheritance, and perhaps—she'd been thinking about this lately—even if she did. But that could wait for another time. Other matters demanded her attention.

"Mary Jill, *chérie*, we're making a mess here. Will you get me that cookbook again, please?"

The child nodded her blond head once and got down off the stool Sabre had pulled up to the counter for her. Her tennis shoes squeaked across the tile floor. A chair screeched as she pushed it away from the table. Her flowered shorts peeking out from beneath the tail of a pink tank top, she stretched her slender arms across the Formica tabletop and grasped the heavy book in small, sticky hands.

Sabre smiled, watching her. She really was a lovely child, all ribbons and bows and fine, yellow hair. She seemed younger than her eight years, slightly immature both physically and emotionally, the result, no doubt, of doting parents. Yet Sabre thought she was the happiest, most friendly child she had ever met, and she so obviously adored Theo, her "great-gumpa," and was adored, in turn, by him. Unfortunately, Theo had had to go out for a bit. Mallory had sent him on some urgent errand, something about her women's club. He had asked Sabre to entertain his little Mary Jill, saying that the child had formed a genuine attachment to her, but Sabre couldn't imagine this particular girl not loving anyone freely and wholeheartedly. It made her wonder what was wrong with bitter, unloving Jeanetta and why the two of them had never been able to find some common ground. Maybe it wasn't Jeanetta. Maybe it was her, Sabre. Maybe there was something wrong with her—and she wasn't thinking just of Jeanetta Goula, anymore. Sweet heaven, how the list had grown since she'd come here!

In the beginning, she'd thought that, like Mary Jill, she could make certain people love her. God knew she was willing to love them, couldn't stop herself, in fact. But that didn't seem to matter, not to Grandfather, not to Mallory—and certainly not to Kenyon Ames. Oh, he had explained it quite carefully. She had agreed quite stoically— what else could she do?—that romance was out of the question and, ever since, her "very good friend" had been teaching her just how miserable she could be.

It would have been better if they didn't spend so much time together, but how else, he had said, could he teach her the social skills she needed to know? And so they had sped up the schedule. She had gone to dinners with him, magnificent places where the waiters wore cropped jackets and crystal glittered on every table. She had eaten dishes she'd never heard of and been tested with rows of silverware and glasses in the process. They had practiced introductions, with Kenyon singling out a broad variety of persons with whom to test her memory and use of the proper forms of address. He called these exercises her "unofficial introductions" into society and pointed out that she should have been thrilled because she had done so well. She had smiled and pretended carefree delight, praying that the "instruction" would stop. It did not.

They had gone to ridiculous places, like the airport and the theatre, just so he could instruct her how to tip and how to make an entrance and how to ask for assistance she didn't need. He'd told her silly stories, always with a point, explained why this was the done thing and that was not, however more sense the opposite seemed to make. He'd cautioned her not to speak of the bayou and her experiences there for fear of seeming "foreign" or "low" in exalted company. They'd made trips to the library, which Sabre loved, in order to list the types of books that were acceptable for "public" discussion. Over a period of time, they compiled lists on other acceptable subjects—movies, plays, fashion designers and artists—as well as a variety of *un*acceptable topics: religion, politics, finance and crime, to name a few. It was some education he had given her, a crash course in snobbery and pretense, and almost every moment of it had been pure hell.

She sighed, her thoughts glum and heavy. If only she could go home again, but to what? To whom? She couldn't allow Butler to support her, and if she hadn't known it before, she now knew she couldn't allow Ami Goula to do so, either. But what, exactly, did she hope to accomplish here? She wasn't certain any longer. She only knew that somewhere in this world there had to be a place where she truly belonged, one little spot all her own. She remembered an advertisement she'd read in the newspaper that morning for a live-in sitter, but then Mary Jill tugged on her apron string, and she remembered the real sitting job she'd been given.

Mary Jill had taken the time to look up the recipe herself, remembering the pictures used for illustration. Sabre laughed despite herself, and her mood correspondingly

lightened. Putting away her dark thoughts, she managed to
concentrate well enough to find what she needed.

"Ah," she said, reading aloud, "if mixture is too thin,
thicken with confectioner's sugar." She smiled at Mary Jill
and went to search the shelf where Theo kept the dry food-
stuffs. She found a four-pound bag and carried it into the
kitchen, but while she was looking for the scissors with
which to cut it open, Mary Jill presented her with a sealed,
plastic container.

"I think Great-Gumpa uses this one," she said, and Sabre
stared at her mournfully.

"Of course, he does," she said, at last, going down on
one knee. "Mary Jill, I'm sorry. I'm not much fun this afternoon, am I?" The child hugged the plastic box.

"I get sad sometimes, too," she said knowingly, and
Sabre ruffled her puffy bangs.

"A pretty thing like you should never be sad."

The child beamed at her. "But I'm not as pretty as you
are!"

Sabre laughed. "What a lovely thing to say."

"And quite impossible to believe," said a drawling voice.
Sabre turned and found Kenyon lounging at the end of the
counter. He was wearing a blue shirt striped thinly in yellow and cuffed, navy blue slacks. Funny how she remembered nearly every article in his closet but didn't even
recognize half the things in her own. The shirt was open at
the throat, and he held a lightweight, navy blue cardigan in
one hand.

"Mary Jill," Sabre murmured, "I want you to meet Mr.
Ames. He's a...friend. Mary Jill is Theo's great-
granddaughter."

Kenyon came forward and bowed. Mary Jill giggled.
"Pleased to meet you, Mr. Ames."

"Pleased to meet you, Mary Jill. Now come here and let's
settle who's prettier, shall we?" She joyfully allowed her-

self to be lifted and set on the counter. Kenyon pretended to study them, looking from one to the other. "Hmm." Sabre felt the sharpness of his gaze and looked away, discomfitted by this sudden appearance. He tickled Mary Jill with his exaggerated perusal, milked it for all it was worth, and finally made his pronouncement. "Nope," he stated flatly. "You're wrong. You're every bit as pretty as Sabre is and, my sweet, that's saying something."

Sabre didn't know quite how to take the compliment, but the frank gaze he settled on her seemed to say that he was sincere. She thanked him, and he made the standard reply, then winked and clasped his hands behind his back, his attention focused fully on her. An awkward moment passed, then he snapped his fingers and launched into merry conversation.

"Want to go for a trolley ride?"

"Mary Jill and I are waiting for Theo to return."

"Oh," he said brightly. "I'll wait with you, then."

"Well, we're making cookies," she explained haltingly, but he remained undaunted.

"Great!" He smacked his hands and rubbed them together.

Irritated, Sabre turned away. Patiently, she instructed Mary Jill to measure the powdered sugar and stir it into the little pots of edible paint they'd made, then turned her attention back to Kenyon.

"Honestly, Kenyon," she told him, keeping her voice low, "I don't feel much like the dutiful student today."

"Who said anything about lessons? In fact, Miss Callot, today I am giving you your sheepskin." He held out his hands, both brows arched expectantly, but she could only stare. "Don't you get it?" he asked. "Teacher says you've passed with flying colors. The diploma's in the mail."

Sabre put a wrist to her head, trying to think of a polite acknowledgment, but a cold dark feeling had settled over her. She knew what was coming next. She put on a limp smile and decided to save him the trouble.

"That's great," she said. "I guess you'll be going home now." The expression on his face changed very little, but the color seemed to drain away. She knew he was feeling guilty.

"Not right away," he said, "but soon."

Her heart was beating slowly and painfully, but she brightened her smile and dusted her hands, prepared to put a quick end to it. She had known, after all, that the moment would come, had spent countless hours dreading and planning for it. In parting, she must convince him how very much in control of her feelings she was. It was her parting gift to him.

"I don't know how to thank you, Kenyon," she said evenly. "You've been the dearest of friends. *Grand merci, cher ami.*" She carefully took his face in her hands and placed a delicate kiss on the corner of his mouth. *"Bon voyage."* She smiled and turned away and began to pat the mound of dough on the counter, apparently calm, as if cookies were the only thing on her mind.

He stood there a few moments longer. "I...you're a very special woman, Sabre."

Why must he go through the motions? she thought. *Isn't it enough that I'm bleeding inside? Must I bleed outwardly for him?* She shot him a smile.

"You don't have to say these things, *mon ami.* After all that you've done, what could you possibly add? Be glad for me, eh? I am a new woman, thanks to you."

"There wasn't really anything wrong with the old Sabre," he commented quietly, and she laughed, hoping the note of bitterness didn't ring through.

"No? Nothing except ignorance, eh? Even Mallory now says that occasionally—only occasionally, mind you—poor breeding can be overcome."

"That's a cruel, tasteless remark," he said acidly.

"A lesson from the student, *mon cher*," she replied mildly. "One of the first things I learned here was how acceptable cruelty and tastelessness can be. One needs only the correct words and tone." She worked the dough, carefully guiding a wooden rolling pin over the growing circle. "Have you chosen a cutter?" she asked, addressing Mary Jill. The child nodded enthusiastically. "Here, let me help you. Where's your paint brush, hmm?" It was easy to smile at the girl, easier than to face Kenyon.

"I'm sorry it's been so difficult for you, Sabre," he said with much feeling. "I only wish... That is, I hope everything turns out the way you want it to."

What she wanted at the moment was for him to go, but she couldn't say so. That would have been honest and obvious, thoroughly unacceptable. Oh, what she had given to learn that. She pushed the cookie cutter down into the dough and jiggled it gently.

"Don't worry about me, Kenyon," she said. "Whatever happens, I'm going to be just fine. I have plans for my future, you know. That's why, no matter what Grandfather decides, I'm going to repay your sponsorship money. I'm going to make it in this new world you've opened for me, Kenyon, never fear."

"I don't want repayment, Sabre," he told her softly. "In fact, I don't want—"

"Oh, Mr. Kenyon, you're here. I take it you got the message, sir." It was Theo, his arms full of packages, the flat, jaunty cap he liked to wear when out-of-doors still atop his head. He dumped the packages on the table, removed the cap and quickly peeled off his lightweight jacket. "Mary Jill, my love, how are you doing?" He gave the child a quick hug and turned back to the adults. "I was so worried, Mr. Kenyon. Those infernal answering machines. I called twice, sir, because I wasn't certain I'd reached the correct number the first time. One can't ask questions of a recording, you know."

Sabre had a question of her own, just then. She looked from Theo to Kenyon to Theo, again. "What's going on?"

"I don't really know, Miss Sabre," Theo answered briskly, beginning to tidy up. "Just as I was leaving earlier, Mr. Van asked me to notify Mr. Kenyon and you that he wants to see the pair of you in his room first thing after lunch."

"It's the other reason I'm here," Kenyon told her cautiously. "I thought you might know what it's about."

Sabre could only shake her head in puzzlement. "No, I'm sorry. This is the first I've heard of it."

"Well, I'm sure it's nothing to worry about." She smiled lamely and went back to watching Mary Jill paint a cookie shaped like a toy locomotive. Kenyon cleared his throat. "I thought we could have lunch together."

"Oh, yes, you two do that," Theo urged. "Mary Jill and I will finish up here."

A feeling of hopelessness swept over her as she searched for a way to decline, but even as she stalled, she knew she would have to go. To do otherwise would raise all sorts of questions she felt inadequate to answer.

"I have to change," she mumbled, making for the door, but Kenyon stopped her with a hand at her wrist.

"You look great."

She shook her head, deftly extracting herself from his grip. "Aunt Mallory won't like it if I go out in jeans. I won't be long."

"No, really," he said, surprising her with the determination in his tone. "I thought we'd go to the park, grab a couple of hot dogs, just keep it casual, you know?"

Whatever was he thinking? she wondered. Keeping it casual wasn't in the repertoire. She put on her most imperious smile. "I'll be right back," she said, and made her exit swiftly.

She didn't want to think about what was coming. It did no good to wonder what her grandfather might be up to, and she couldn't maintain composure dwelling on what might be her last moments with Kenyon Ames. It wasn't too difficult to keep her mind off those unpleasant thoughts. She had to decide what to wear, after all. Choosing the correct garment for the occasion was a mark of the well-educated, well-bred woman, wasn't it?

She chose a pair of pleated khaki slacks and a loose, white, unstructured jacket with padded shoulders and no lapels to go with the blouse she was already wearing. A narrow belt at the waist, a scarf knotted about her neck, and a pair of tan moccasin flats completed the ensemble. As they were going to the park, she left the tasteful gold button earrings and matching sweater pin in the jewelry box.

Kenyon commented that she had chosen well when she returned to him in the kitchen, but she knew she had, and therefore, the compliment felt small and unimportant. Perhaps, she thought, that was a good sign. Perhaps she was *not* in love with Kenyon Ames, after all. They went out by way of the carriage-house portal and caught the trolley going uptown toward Audubon Park, four-hundred acres of outdoor recreation area located across from the campuses of Loyola and Tulane universities, the city's most famous next-door neighbors.

They avoided the golf links, tennis courts, horseback-riding trails, playgrounds and zoo, to wander in the quiet gardens beneath stately oaks and munch hot dogs purchased from a street vendor. Kenyon was in an oddly playful mood, not at all his usual serious self, while Sabre was somber and pensive and oh so very proper. He laughed and made light of the past weeks, seeming all the while to be dancing around some deeper, weightier subject, until Sabre decided to do the done thing and close this chapter with grace and aplomb. They stopped at a cast-iron bench curved around an ancient tree, and sat side by side but not touching. Sabre chose the moment.

"Kenyon, *bon ami*, about that evening at your borrowed apartment..."

Kenyon looked down at the soft-drink cup in his hand. "I'm glad you brought that up."

"I've been meaning to for a while," she said, getting up to circle the tree. "I wanted to tell you how glad I am—" She paused to take a deep breath "—that you were so sensible that night. I was so lonely and lost and...foolish, and you were so kind and gentle and—"

"Foolish," he said from the other side of the tree. She heard him get up, and had just a moment to prepare herself before he stepped around to join her. She turned away and reached overhead to feel the rough bark on a low hanging limb. "Sabre," he said, his tone so earnest it wounded her, "you'll never know how I regret—"

"Yes," she interrupted smoothly, "I regret my part in that *embrouillement*, too." She made herself look at him, her gaze level and unflinching. "That's why I'm so very grateful, you see, that you were good enough to correct the situation."

He opened his mouth as if to speak, then seemed to think better of it and reformulated. "Well," he said, "I'm glad I somehow managed to do the right thing."

A bird chirped overhead somewhere, and Sabre all too eagerly seized the diversion. They spent several moments trying to spy the little musician, Sabre with more interest than she felt, Kenyon with less enthusiasm than he might have. Sabre chalked up his lack of zeal to an impatience to be away, perhaps even to boredom, and he did nothing to dispel that impression when she suggested they give up the hunt and return to Garrick House.

The mood was definitely muted on the return trip, but both had a ready explanation for their somber attitude. A meeting with Vanguard Garrick invariably became an interview, if not an interrogation, and this one was to be no exception.

Van Garrick was up and sitting in a wheelchair beside his bed when they entered his chamber. Beneath his red velvet dressing gown, the hems of a pair of gray slacks were visible, hanging above thin ankles clad also in gray and a pair of highly polished black shoes. Mallory stood at his shoulder, straight and rather sinister-looking. The gargoyle protecting the icon, thought Sabre. Darryl leaned an elbow against the mantel, looking very much like the cat who had swallowed the canary.

"Ah, the pupil and her tutor," said the cat.

"Mind your mouth," said the master.

Sabre bowed her head. "Grandfather. It's good to see you up for a change."

"Oh, I've been up and about a good bit," he said. "The chariot here helps, and as the spirit has risen of late, I've decided the time has come to put my potential heirs to test."

Sabre mentally sighed. *One more hurdle,* she thought. *But my heart's no longer in the race.* Kenyon's supportive hand settled in the small of her back, adding a solemn poignancy to the moment. She took a deep breath, but found it not particularly fortifying. Her grandfather was speaking.

"... different areas, of course. That's to be expected. So, Darryl has been given a small business deal to work out. Nothing major, you understand. I'm not about to risk any real capital. But it has potential, and it will be informative to see what he makes of it." Darryl indulged in a confident smirk, but Sabre was far beyond caring what Darryl Garrick thought about anything.

"You presented a problem for me, Sabre," Van went on, "until Mallory came up with a suitable idea." *That* was not particularly comforting, but the emotional malaise in which she found herself would not allow it to be particularly threatening, either.

"And what would Aunt Mallory's idea be?" she heard herself asking in a rather skeptic voice. Van Garrick smiled, obviously pleased with the notion.

"A dinner party, my dear, to celebrate the improvement in my health, modest though it may be."

A small, feral smile curved Mallory's stern mouth. She clasped her hands together, then parted them. "Nothing terribly complicated," she said in an oddly throaty voice. "I'll give you a list of people you are to invite. We've agreed, brother and I, on those who simply must be included. It will top out around two dozen, I think. Theo and the cook can help you with the menu. Six courses sounds appropriate, maybe seven. After-dinner entertainment will be left to you. Again, Theo can tell you what has been done in the past. Try not to be repetitive. The occasion calls for something original, I think." She paused to pass a hand over her brother's shoulder and was rewarded with a thin smile before getting back to business. "You'll have a budget, of course. In fact, I'm opening a special account for you today. You can handle a checkbook?"

The question seemed ludicrous to Sabre. A checkbook? She should worry about handling a checkbook when she was expected to organize an entire dinner party? Just a little affair, of course—for twenty-four! With entertainment, yet! And do be original, darling. Sabre chuckled.

"Oh, Aunt Mallory," she said, and the disconcerted look on the old woman's face seemed purely comical. Sabre laughed outright, and the reaction that brought seemed funnier still. Kenyon's hand slid around her waist and dug into her side, not merely supportive any longer.

"I hope I'm on the list!" he said brightly, while Sabre recovered herself. Mallory blanched. Sabre lifted a quizzical brow.

"I thought you were going back to Houston."

"Airplanes fly both ways," he said. "Besides, I have a bit of business demanding a return."

"How wonderful," Mallory observed, her tone too bright to mean anything but the opposite. "Well, of course, it's only fitting that you should witness the *coup de maître* for which you've prepared your pupil."

"Or the *défaut misérable*," put in Darryl.

Kenyon telegraphed him a fixed smile. "I have every confidence in Sabre. I'm very much looking forward to the occasion. Just see that you don't get in her way, cousin Garrick. We have a saying in Texas: Damn the odds, just level the playing field. I think your uncle would agree with that sentiment."

"Quite," Van Garrick affirmed. "That is precisely why I must stress that this is Sabre's project and Sabre's alone." He leaned forward, elbows braced against the arms of his chair. "We appreciate the assistance you have given in the past, Ames, and we look forward to seeing you again." It was an unmistakable dismissal.

Kenyon drew himself up and nodded slowly. "My pleasure, sir." He targeted Darryl, his gaze hard and pointed. "I look forward to my return." When he turned to Sabre, she felt the sharp wrench of parting, but the smile he had for her was tender and warm and encouraging. He curled a finger beneath her chin, tipping her face to hold it for a moment with his blue gaze, as if memorizing the features. "I believe the phrase is *bonne chance*," he said softly, and he drew her gently to him, pressing his lips to the smooth plain of her brow before slipping from the room.

Chapter Nine

One more time, Theo," Sabre said, running down the list in her notebook. "Bar will open at seven-ten p.m. The aperitif tray will appear at exactly 7:30, and the hors d'oeuvres will be ready by?"

"Seven-forty, miss."

"First course to be served at?"

"Eight-twenty."

"Second course?"

"Eight-thirty-five."

"Third?"

"Eight-fifty."

"Fourth?"

"Nine-ten, Miss, and fifth comes in at precisely nine-thirty, with the sixth served as an accompaniment immediately after. Dessert will be served in two courses beginning at ten."

"You're a wonder, Theo, a treasure," she said, flipping

the page. "Now let's go down the beverage list, shall we? Everything should be in house by now."

Theo reached across the kitchen table and gently closed the binder spread out before his young mistress. "It's done, Miss Sabre. I went over it myself not an hour ago. The liqueurs, the spirits, the wines, all here. Everything's here, Miss Sabre: antipasto, vegetables, breads, meats—"

"But not the lobsters?" she said in horror. Theo smiled and shook his head sadly.

"Not the lobsters, miss. They'll be delivered live at eight-thirty, and I've already deputized a cook's helper to wait for and receive them."

"Oh, that reminds me, Theo. About the additional staff—"

"Cook is already here, with one helper. Another comes in at three o'clock. Bartender will arrive at six. Waiters come in at six-thirty and will remain after dinner to help clean up. Cook refuses to help clean—he's an artist, you know—so, he'll be off as soon as the Baked Alaska is out of the oven. Let's see, have we forgotten anything? Ah. The florist will deliver at five-fifteen." Sabre opened her mouth, but he was one step ahead of her. "That's eight arrangements, three at table, two in the drawing room, one in the salon, and two for the main hall, or rather, the theatre. I'll personally arrange the table, with a full compliment, I promise, and you may check it at six-thirty, if that's all right with you."

Sabre sat back with a satisfied sigh and smiled. "Theo, I love you."

"If that's true," the elderly houseman told her, "you'll relax and pamper yourself the whole rest of this day. You've been working much too hard, Miss Sabre, for more'n three weeks, and tonight's your big night. If you don't get some rest, you're not even going to enjoy it."

Sabre laughed ruefully. "Theo, I'll be more than happy just to survive this evening. Besides, I still have so much to do."

"Well, while you're doin', miss, why don't you try to find time to return Mr. Ames's phone call? He called again this morning first thing, and I told him you were awful busy, but I could tell he was a mite disappointed."

Sabre stood and gathered up her notebook. So he had called again, had he? She supposed he thought it was the done thing for an out-of-town guest to do, and it probably was, but she didn't want to talk to him. He had been in town for two or three days already. Mallory had seen him in the company of Alfred Pantier and a woman named Karen Cromier.

"I wouldn't put it past him," Mallory had said, "to try to wrangle an invitation for that Karen."

Perhaps it was foolish of her to be hurt because Kenyon had been in town several days and only last evening had bothered to call, but she couldn't help it. A good friend, it seemed, would have phoned sooner. Not that it mattered, she reminded herself. She almost wished he wouldn't come. It would be easier not to have to see him again. And yet . . . It was awful to have these mixed feelings about everyone and everything. She straightened her spine and thumped the table top with a manicured forefinger.

"If Mr. Ames calls again," she said dismissively, "tell him I'll see him this evening. Now if we're to have entertainment tonight, I've really got to see that everything is kept on schedule."

Theo shook his head. "I swear, Miss Sabre, you're as bad as your great-aunt Mallory, when it comes to keeping your hand in. Never leave nothing to chance, that's her motto. Ride ever' horse to a standstill. Made in her mold, I guess. She's always the most organized—"

"That will be quite enough!"

She realized, the instant the words were out, what she'd done, and the look on his face told her she'd done a good job of it, too. He was right, more right than even he had known. She was like Mallory. At least she was becoming like Mallory, and the tone she had just used with him proved it. Suddenly, they were no longer friends, compatriots working at parallel purposes, but mistress and servant. Sabre bit her lip, ashamed and appalled, ashamed that the insult she had felt in his comparison of her to her aunt had caused her to snap at him in that imperious tone, ashamed that her reaction had proven the comparison apt.

"Oh, Theo, *cher ami*, I'm so sorry. I didn't mean it the way it sounded."

"That's all right, Miss Sabre. I was running off at the mouth, and you're so tired."

"I am tired, Theo," she admitted bitterly. "Tired of this life I'm leading, tired of trying to be someone I'm not."

"There now," he said, rising and reaching across the table for her hand. "You'll feel better once this dinner party is over. You aren't yourself, right now."

"No, I'm not," she agreed, but this wasn't the time for breaking down. Tomorrow. Tomorrow she would think about who she was and who she really wanted to be and what to do. Tomorrow.

The theatrical troop arrived well before lunch and began setting up in the main hall. This part of her plans, Sabre had kept a deep mystery from everyone but Theo, who had not only approved but applauded her creativity. She had gotten the idea from a book at the library about the early days of radio, complete with a sample script of a series' episode, elaborate details on the creation of sound effects, pictures and a list of original sponsors. She had been fascinated, and it wasn't long afterward while shopping in the Vieux Carré in the early evening, that she had come upon a quartet of street players doing a broadly satirical version of *Romeo and Juliet* for the early-dinner crowd at a sidewalk café. Seeing that they worked for what they could collect from their "patrons," she had the bright idea that they might like a real paying job for a change, and she hadn't been wrong. The moment she'd laid out her proposal, they'd started brainstorming. Within the hour she'd had a deal, a partial script, a list of recordings to purchase, and a sketch of a stage setting. It had been a small matter to rent the few necessary props, particularly the old-fashioned sound-effects devices and a microphone. The actors were providing their own costumes and the labor for constructing the small stage. Now if everything would only go according to plan.

It was a good idea, recreating a "live" radio broadcast from the 1930s, certainly an original one, but Sabre couldn't help feeling the cold hand of doom. She tried not to give credence to the perception of threat, but her father had long held to the idea that certain Cajun folk possessed an ill-defined sixth sense, and for the first time, she wondered if she might have that so-called gift. The feeling of imminent failure had driven her to be organized to the point of obsession, and while she liked the new her to a degree, she was also frightened of her. She didn't want to be like Mallory, but she didn't want to be the old Sabre, either. The answer was, of course, to be a different woman, to have some of the new, some of the old, some yet to be, but she couldn't think of that now. Funny how life could be lived only a day, an hour, a moment at a time. Things hadn't changed so very much from the bayou, after all.

She was tired, worn clear through, by midafternoon, but it was only Theo's renewed insistence that made her retire to her room for a much-needed soak in the pink tub. Of all the luxuries of Garrick House, it was the private bath that she relished most. She had discovered that a good, long soak was the most relaxing of activities, and after forty minutes of letting steaming water go tepid, she felt like a newborn at nap time. She drifted off for an hour of undisturbed sleep, waking to the soft, golden light of early evening. She felt fine upon arising, but by half past six she was as nervous as a mouse in a cat's paw.

She changed clothes three times and then changed again, back into the sleek black dress she'd chosen originally. She wore earrings for the first time in her life, heavy gold hoops an inch wide, and a thick gold chain from which she removed a 1960's peace symbol. As an afterthought, she added a wide gold wrist band with her mother's name engraved on it.

Mallory had snidely recommended a hairdresser a long time ago, it seemed, but Sabre was nervous about going to one. What if she hated what he'd done with her hair? What if she came out looking like one of those punk-rockers she saw on television? She had taken Mallory's advice on another matter, however, and had her nails done by an extraordinary young woman who'd come to the house. *Her* advice had been to stick with the familiar and save experimentation for a day when she wouldn't have to make any public appearances she didn't want to, and that made up her mind for her. Just as she'd done the very day of her arrival, she brushed her hair until it gleamed like satin, then carefully rolled the sides up, and pinned them in place atop her head, leaving the back to fall over her shoulders. Then, in the dainty black shoes Kenyon had told her were appropriate for the dress and the black silk stockings that made her feel like the most pampered of princesses, she went out to check the table setting and oversee any final details until the arrival of the first of her guests.

They numbered twenty-four, counting Kenyon, each confirmed in writing as well as by telephone, making a total of twenty-eight for dinner, adding the four residents of Garrick House. The early arrivals were all contemporaries of her grandfather and aunt, and among them she felt like a child allowed to sit with the adults before being shuttled off to bed, especially when she overheard Mallory saying, "A real babe in the woods, our Sabre, completely out of her milieu, poor dear. I hope the evening won't be a disappointment. Of course, she had Theo to help her. Dear Theo, what would we do without him?" The conversation wandered off after that, but Sabre was now fully aware that nothing she did would work for her benefit, as far as her aunt was concerned. Should the night be a success, the credit would undoubtedly be all Theo's. Nevertheless, the moment demanded her attention, and she gave it that in full measure.

As hostess, it was her responsibility to greet the guests, make a place for them among the others, see that they were served with drinks and comfortably engaged in interesting conversation, then gracefully disengage herself to tend a myriad of other chores. It should have been a relief to find herself taking a familiar arm for a change, but her need to protect herself from her feelings for Kenyon was so strong that she found his arrival in the company of the Pantiers disturbing rather than comforting.

"You're nervous," he said, as she led him toward the others.

"Do I seem nervous?" she asked, keeping her tone light and her smile intact.

"No," he assured her, all charm and grace, "but I can feel you trembling—or is that latent desire?" He said it jokingly, but her breath caught, all the same, and for an instant she felt exposed, found out. The next moment she'd regained her equilibrium and sent him a sharp, unamused glare. The response was a quirky grimace. "That's been happening a good deal lately," he said with a sigh. "Call it poor timing, a poor choice of words, poor taste. You choose."

"I hardly think I'm qualified," she told him through her teeth. "You're a good teacher, Kenyon, but you forget that I was raised in the bayou. It seems we're short on the social graces there. You've made that obvious, all of you." She lifted a hand and swept it in a wide arc, as if bidding him to join their friendly party. He lowered his eyes and pressed the hand she had tucked beneath his elbow to his side.

"We're a pack of asses," he said flatly and, though surprised, she put on a benign smile and gave a small nod.

"Yes, you are," she agreed, without so much as a break in stride. Her smile brightened as they neared the first cluster of guests, and she mentally noted that she had learned some lessons very well, indeed.

Within moments she had installed Kenyon next to an elderly woman discussing the report, on good authority, that the Russian ambassador who had recently toured their city was nearly crippled with bunions on his toes and plantar warts. It was an interesting bit of intelligence, but Sabre couldn't stay around for the ensuing speculation about why he didn't defect to Sweden and let one of their excellent surgeons operate on his feet.

The last guests arrived just as a young, white-coated waiter appeared with the aperitifs—apricot brandy mulled with cinnamon in tiny stemmed glasses. The hors d'oeuvres came in right behind, as planned, and Sabre silently commended her help with a couple of judicious nods and smiles. The elderly merely sniffed and nibbled, but they praised the choice and taste of the offerings. The younger, ranging in age from twenty-five to fifty-five, literally gobbled. Like all New Orleanians, they prided themselves on their appreciation of good food. Sabre stole a moment to kiss Theo's cheek in thanks, but she was all too aware of the many pitfalls that lay ahead.

Using Mallory's information about who detested whom and who ought not to be seen monopolizing one another's company in public and who simply adored chitchat and who never spoke on any subject but business, Sabre had carefully arranged a seating chart. One part of her deeply feared failure at this juncture, while another wanted to throw up her hands and tell the lot of them to just grow up and eat their dinners. She managed, however, to remain charmingly aloof and to smile and behave graciously when her grandfather insisted she wheel him into the dining room, causing Mallory to glare daggers at her. Sabre had no idea whether the honor of assisting Grandfather was bestowed as a reward for partial success or as a test, but she didn't have time to worry about it.

Wisely, she had positioned her grandfather at the head of the immense banquet table and her aunt at its foot. She had chosen center chairs on opposite sides of the table for herself and Kenyon, being careful that they weren't placed directly across from one another, a decision she now appreciated. At first it was difficult to keep her attention from wandering constantly to his seat, but more immediate matters soon presented themselves.

Her two closest dinner companions were a pair of octogenarian males. The one on her left was nearly deaf and seemed content to pick at his food in silence, nodding at Sabre whenever she chose to bend close to his ear and pass on some bit of conversation. The other, however, was all too frisky. He used every opportunity to touch her. His hoary hand kept landing on her knee, and no matter how often or how firmly she removed it, it kept coming back again. Her patience was wearing thin when Kenyon caught her eye, his left brow rising in pointed question. She answered with a deep breath and a thin smile, never hoping that he might correctly divine her situation.

Almost instantly, Kenyon raised a hand and brought a young waiter to his side. One quiet word brought an immediate reply, then the young man stepped off toward the kitchen. At once, Theo appeared in the doorway. Sabre took the time to follow his gaze. It went straight to Kenyon, who gave a barely perceptible nod and switched his attention pointedly to Sabre. It was precisely then that her aged masher resumed his press, and she left one mystery to deal with another. What, she wondered, did this frail, old man hope to gain with his pestering? She couldn't believe how calmly he ate with his right hand, while with his left he doggedly attempted to explore her thigh!

It was difficult to keep her mind on her duties, but the very instant the first waiter strode through the door with an oval covered dish balanced expertly on an upturned palm, she knew they'd skipped a course. When he came immediately to her side, her *right* side, she knew it had been no accident. As the succulent lobster was laid before her and the polished silver dome was taken away, she knew she had been rescued. No one could eat this large, lovely crustacean without *two* hands. She sent a quick glance at the doorway, where Theo bowed and smiled and indicated with a purposeful wave that the credit was to be shared. She looked at Kenyon Ames, who made a discreet show of taking tongs and fork in hand. She gave him a languid salute. *Merci, mon ami*, she told him with her eyes, and the slight inclination of his head told her the message was received and understood.

The remainder of the meal passed in relative ease. An odd sense of well-being had settled over her, and her rescuers saw to it that she was not bothered again. Every time her lecherous companion raised his head, a waiter appeared to inquire his pleasure. "More coffee, sir? More water? A touch of wine, perhaps? A second helping?" One guest would leave the table thinking the service obsequious to the point of harassment, but he wouldn't again find time to press his unwanted attention upon his young hostess. When sufficient time had passed to count everyone done, Sabre

hecked up and down the table, then nodded a signal to her
randfather, who rapped his wineglass with a spare spoon.

"Ladies and gentlemen," he said, "along with this ex-
ellent meal, my granddaughter has arranged entertain-
ent for us. If you will repair to the salon, we'll enjoy a cup
f coffee, then make our way to the ballroom, where I'm
old we have a genuine treat waiting."

General statements of approval and appreciation were
udible above the sounds of departure, rufflings and scrap-
gs, subdued laughter, tiny clinks and clanks. One of the
aiters assigned the post of watchdog held Sabre's chair for
er and effectively blocked the path of her nemesis until she
ad safely availed herself of the arm of her deaf compan-
on. As she passed the end of the table, Kenyon managed to
all in behind her, a painfully thin middle-aged woman on
is arm.

"My congratulations," he said quite near her ear. "I be-
eve you've managed—what is the term?—a *coup d'état*."

She was amused by his pronunciation as well as his choice
f phrase. "And you, sir, pulled off a clear *coup de grâce*,"
he told him. "Thank you."

"My pleasure," he replied. "Friends?"

She bowed her head, wondering how wise it would be to
ive in to the impulse to say yes. She hesitated, her escort
equiring a moment to adjust himself from movement
cross carpet to movement across marble, and Kenyon
wept his charge past her, allowing her no time for reply. She
ecided instantly that it was for the best.

Upon entering the salon, she found Mallory informing
veryone that they'd missed a course at dinner.

"Well, I for one didn't miss it," Kenyon said loudly. "I
hought the dinner was excellent. My compliments to the
hef."

Several others agreed, but Mallory looked piqued.
"Theo," she called to the elderly houseman as he entered the

room with the coffee tray, "we were a course short at din
ner. What have you to say about it?"

Sabre could see all of her hard work going right down the
drain, but she lifted her chin, aware of her aunt's pointe
glance. She expected Theo to stutter and stumble and fi
nally come out with the unsavory truth, but she needn't hav
worried. Theo, dear Theo, lied like a rug on the floor.

"It was the meat salad, madam," he said evenly. "Mis
Sabre inspected it earlier and found it was off. I can't imag
ine what went wrong. We used the usual butcher, the on
you favor, but the meat was definitely off. Thanks to Mis
Sabre, it was discovered in time."

From failure to heroine in one fell swoop. Mallory looke
as if she'd just heard an unsatisfactory weather report, bu
everyone else heaped praise on the revealed heroine. It wa
all Sabre could do to keep from bursting out with laughter
especially when Kenyon gave her a surreptitious thumbs u
sign and Theo simultaneously offered her dinnertim
masher a cup of dangerously hot coffee. But a catastroph
averted didn't provide insurance against the next, and th
longer she had to look at Mallory's sour face, the more sh
wondered if she wouldn't have been better off to settle for
little light music and a game of cards instead of trying t
stage a period radio broadcast for entertainment. She sus
pected both Mallory and Darryl would openly celebrate he
downfall, and the wicked grin on Darryl's face seeme
nothing less than confirmation.

It was far too late for second thoughts, however. Withi
half an hour, the company was once again on the move. Sh
found herself on the arm of another elderly gentleman, he
anxiety growing with each and every step. She had appro
priated the area known as the main hall for her program. I
was a large expanse of open space flanking the stairwell. A
set of large double-pocket doors separated it from the spa
cious parlor. When open, those doors transformed parlo

and hall into ballroom. At the moment, however, the hall was a theatre, complete with chairs, and the parlor functioned as dressing room and wings.

As soon as the assembled guests were seated, a man in Thirties costume, a cigar jammed between his teeth, entered and began to direct them as if they were a bona fide audience at a radio broadcast. He laid down the rules for them: No crying babies. No obscene noises or speaking. No coming and going during broadcast, as indicated by a red light bulb mounted above the fabricated broadcast booth. Laughter was permitted when a proper response, as well as applause and the occasional gasp. Sabre heard one elderly guest whisper to another, "Just like the old days!" It was the first indication of what was to be a roaring success.

When it was all over, the critics raved. Even Mallory had been entertained, though it obviously pained her royally to say so. Guests and drinks were brought into the drawing room, and the doors to the garden were opened. Thirties music was playing softly on an old Victrola she had rented from a theatrical-supply company. Sabre was a great success, and yet she felt oddly hollow, detached from the whole affair and utterly exhausted.

Taking advantage of a quiet moment, she slipped outside into the garden, but several guests had gathered there to talk, cousin Darryl among them. Making her excuses, she strolled away from them, down the path that ran along the front of the house to the side, where the old oak stood with her mother's swing in its ancient arms. It felt cool and clean beneath the shady branches. The narrow heels of her shoes sunk deeply into the moist, grassy earth as she walked through the shadows toward the swing. Why had Grandfather kept it hanging all these years? she wondered. Maybe he had just never gotten around to taking it down. In that case, she knew from long experience that the rope would be rotten and soft. Yet, when she took it in hand, it was stiff and prickly and strong. Intrigued, she gave one rope and then the other a hard, sharp tug and found them both sound.

Sabre was bemused. Was it possible that Grandfather had a soft spot, after all; a spot for the little girl his daughter had been? Was it possible, even remotely, that he'd maintained the swing as a sort of memorial for the little girl who had grown up and gone away from him? She pondered that probability and concluded that she was tired and incurably romantic and possibly irrational. Whatever the reason, it wasn't emotional or sentimental, not if her grandfather was involved in it. *Perhaps Theo*, she thought. Yes, that was a good possibility. She would have to remember to ask him.

The seat was thick and wide. She backed up to it and sat down, being careful to position herself so that she wouldn't wrinkle her skirt or snag her stockings. Feeling free, she pushed back and let go, gliding forward effortlessly. The shadows swept by her, and her gaze filled with dappled moonlight. She sighed and let her mind empty of concern. It was so peaceful here, so untroubled.

"Has anyone told you how extraordinarily beautiful you are tonight?"

The voice came out of the dark—smooth, drawling and low—and there wasn't the least doubt to whom it belonged. Sabre caught herself, her heels digging into the ground. Kenyon stepped away from the great, black bulk of the tree trunk, his blond hair darkly silvered against the night. She let her weight down onto the seat, waiting for some great inspiration of wit. It didn't take long to realize it wasn't coming. She finally settled for a polite, "Thank you," and wondered, *Now what?*

Kenyon strolled over to the swing and took hold of the nearest rope with both hands. "You've done really well," he said. "I'm proud of you."

"Well, I had a good teacher," she observed lightly.

He let go of the rope and made a slight, mocking bow. "You know," he said, taking hold of the rope again, "it was kind of fun, wasn't it? I mean, I enjoyed the time we spent together, didn't you?"

She hummed a noncommittal, "hmm." She had liked being with Kenyon. She had even craved his company, and often still did. Yet her time with him usually seemed bittersweet and sometimes even painful. But she couldn't tell him that, and if she could have, it wouldn't have served any purpose. Kenyon had explained his position quite clearly.

He looked up at the strong, thick limb to which the swing was attached and observed, "I guess Mary Jill is the only little girl who swings here now."

Of course. Sabre laughed gently, shaking her head. "Yes," she said, "I suppose she is." The look he gave her meant he hadn't missed the mildly cryptic tone.

"What?" he asked. "Tell me what you're thinking."

"It doesn't matter."

"It does to me."

"Well, it shouldn't."

"But it does," he insisted, reaching down to smooth the back of her hair with one hand.

It was as if he'd pushed a button. One touch from him and her every nerve ending was tingling. She got up hastily and paced beneath the spreading bough.

"This swing used to be my mother's," she said, adopting a conversational tone. "She told me about it long ago, what it was like to swing here, her dreams."

"I see," he said, stepping in front of the seat and sitting down. "This was a special place for her, and so it's a special place for you." He pushed backward with his legs, standing and carrying the swing with him, so that he leaned against it, keeping the ropes taut.

She smiled lamely. "Something like that."

"All right. What's the rest of it?"

She sent him a sharp glance. He had great instinct, this man, but then she hadn't really ever doubted that. She sighed and wandered back to him, thinking she might as well talk about it. What could it hurt? They were friends, weren't they?

"It's silly, I know, but I didn't think about Mary Jill when I first came out here. When I realized the ropes were new, well, I thought Grandfather might have kept it up because of the little girl he'd once had. Her memory, I mean."

He looked down at the ground. The white of his shirt front shone against the black of his tux. "Just can't quite give up, can you?" he asked gently. "If it's any comfort to you, Sabre, I believe that somewhere, deep down under all that severity and gruffness, he does care."

She only looked at him, then shrugged. "There is a saying," she said. "'*Je vis en espoir.* I live in hope.' But…" She shook her head. It was time to face facts. Nothing she had dreamed would happen was going to. She had been foolish, so foolish. She didn't fit in here. She would never fit in here. No matter how hard she tried, she could never be anything more than a pretender, and that wasn't enough. She wanted a life, a real life. It was time to give up the dream and move on to reality. "Never mind," she finished briskly. "I don't want to talk about it, after all."

"Maybe you need to talk about it," he said, but she only shrugged agitatedly.

"I think I should go back inside."

"Not yet," he protested, twisting around to catch her hand. A tiny shock radiated from her palm upward.

"No, really. I'm the hostess, I should go in."

"Why don't you just take a minute."

"I don't think—"

"Sabre, please!"

She tugged at her hand, and he tugged back, perhaps harder than necessary. She jerked forward, catching her heel in the deep turf, and stumbled against him. The blow knocked him off balance. The swing spiraled, the ropes automatically righting themselves. She was falling away from him, but he made a grab for her with both arms, abandoning the swing and coming to his feet. She felt herself caught and reached out for balance. Suddenly they were in each other's arms, the swing bumping and twisting about them.

For a moment she was frozen, experiencing no reaction, at all. Then his hand slid down her back, pushing that button again, and all at once every square inch of her body was clamoring for his touch. She shivered violently, some part of her wanting to throw off the need for him. But his arms tightened about her, and she found herself gazing up into his lean face. Her heart leaped up to her throat, as those gleaming blue eyes moved closer and closer until they seemed to engulf her. His mouth seized hers, his tongue driving her teeth apart, plunging downward to fill the soft, dark cavern inside. She drank the taste of him, absorbed him through her skin, sating needs she didn't recognize, able neither to resist nor to really participate.

She didn't know which of them first realized they weren't alone. All she knew was that someone was there, and suddenly she and Kenyon were breaking apart, turning in concert toward the same spot. Two figures stood at the rim of the shadow of the tree. The red tip of a cigarette brightened and then waned as the smoker exhaled a small cloud of smoke. The pair walked forward at a leisurely pace. Sabre patted her hair, her hands trembling badly.

"Well, this is no surprise." It was Darryl, trying to be smug and friendly at the same time.

"Speak for yourself, Garrick," said the other. "I, for one, am at least mildly shocked." The cigarette glowed again. "Good work, Ken, sly devil."

Kenyon visibly relaxed, his hand going to Sabre's back. "Alfred, it's genetically impossible for a Pantier to be shocked about anything. Now stroll along, will you, and have your smoke elsewhere."

"Hmm, possessive, isn't he?" Darryl observed. "Do I sense a Pygmalion undertone to this little tryst? Or is it simply a matter of picking up where we left off?"

Sabre felt the start of anger in Kenyon's hand, but it was Alfred Pantier who spoke up. "Shove off, Garrick, and shut up."

It was obvious from Darryl's posture that he was incensed, but her cousin was nothing if not prudent. It wouldn't do, as future heir to the Garrick fortune, to incite the disdain of the scion of one of the oldest and most influential families in all of the South. He made a stiff shrug and a quick escape.

"My apologies."

"Man's a mental titmouse," Pantier said after his companion had walked away. "But he's got that Garrick way with a buck. I hear he's made a splash on the business scene, just as you, my dear Sabre, have made a splash on the social scene. My congratulations."

"Thank you," she answered, intending to make her excuses and follow Darryl. Pantier, however, stepped forward, effectively blocking her path.

"Not at all. You know, you might be of service to me," he said, tossing away the cigarette. "I'd like to enlist the aid of your considerable influence on our friend here."

She hadn't the foggiest idea what he was talking about, but Kenyon certainly did. He dropped his hand from Sabre's back and stepped forward almost as if to intervene between her and Pantier.

"Al," he began, "let's not involve Miss Callot."

"Nonsense!" Albert protested good-naturedly. "Truly, dear Sabre, we need him here, don't we? Convince him to stay on."

"Al—"

He waved away the interruption. "A branch office is a good idea, but New Orleans needs his kind of savvy full-time. Houston doesn't appreciate him. It's too big, too urban. Why stop at a branch office when the entire New Orleans legal community—"

"Al, for God's sake!"

"Oh, all right, I'm going—so she can get to work on you. Have fun, kiddies." He strolled away, leaving his friend to face a blank, stunned stare.

"I was going to tell you," Kenyon said apologetically.

"Tell me what?"

"About the new office. It's been a standing offer for some time. He calls it a branch, but it's really a kind of limited partnership. I'll be acting as consultant, really."

"From Houston," she stated flatly, beginning to understand.

"Not entirely. The point is, I just haven't had time to tell you what's been going on."

She wondered suddenly if he'd had time to tell Karen Cromier, but of course he had. It wasn't Karen he'd intended to keep in the dark. She was probably the *right* sort of woman. No bayou stock in her background. What a great inconvenience to be physically attracted to the *wrong* sort of woman, but that didn't really make any difference, did it? Obviously it was Karen Cromier whom he intended to see when he was in town "consulting."

"I don't want to know what's been going on!" she told him fiercely, striding away.

"But, Sabre..." He caught up and reached out a hand, but this time she eluded him.

"Stop it!" she cried, aware that her voice was too loud and immediately attmepting to soften it. "Just stop it. I don't know what you want from me, and I don't think you do, either! But it doesn't matter anymore, Kenyon. It simply doesn't matter."

He looked stricken, positively miserable, his mouth hardening into a grim line.

"I don't blame you," she said. "You can't help what you are any more than I can help what I am." She shook her head sadly. "But it's all right," she told him softly. "Oddly enough, I don't think I want a gentleman for a lover or a friend. At least, with Ami Goula, I know what to expect."

"I'm sorry," he said stiffly. "About what happened back there, I mean."

Sabre sighed. "I'm sorry, too, Kenyon. Now if we could just be sorry about the same thing for once, but we can't seem to do even that much."

They stood staring at one another for some time, neither finding anything to add, until Sabre turned and simply walked away.

Chapter Ten

"Ken."

"Ken."

"Ames!"

"What?" Kenyon bolted upright, his feet crashing to the floor, scattering papers from the corner of his desk. He'd heard his name, but there was no one in his office except... The intercom. He'd done it again, drifted off into his own private little hell while Kathryn needed him. He swiveled in the tan leather chair and reached for the sleek wooden box with all the buttons. He pressed the one that was lit up and leaned forward.

"Kathy?"

"It's about time. I've got all three lines on hold. Carpenter's calling from the courthouse. Munsie's insisting—"

"Forget it, Kat." He rubbed his hand over his face, weary to the very bone. "I can't talk to anyone right now. I'm...busy."

There came a short pause, during which he knew exactly what she was thinking. He was losing it, going right down the tubes, and the worst part was he just couldn't quite make himself give a damn. It all seemed so superficial, so pointless.

"Boss," Kathy's voice said, "at least pick up on three. It's Vanguard Garrick in New—"

He hit the button. "Put him on."

Two seconds later, his phone buzzed. He snatched it up. "Ames."

The smug, familiar voice came through loud and strong. "Mr. Ames. How fortunate to find you in." Kenyon decided to turn on the charm.

"Always have time for you, Van. How are you feeling?"

"Better. Yes, indeed. Better and better."

"That's good, and your sister?"

"Mallory's fine. Mallory's always fine. Remarkable woman, Mallory."

"Indeed. And what of the other lady of the house?"

He heard a chuckle and a pause, and he wanted to bite his tongue. He was being too obvious, much too obvious. On the other hand, why shouldn't he be? What a great fool he'd been, so certain she would fail, so sure she couldn't fit in. Why, just once, couldn't he have followed his heart? He was still kicking himself over the way he'd handled the whole thing from beginning to end. It was the end, wasn't it? Garrick spoke slowly into his ear.

"I assume you are speaking of my granddaughter?"

Kenyon tried to sound lighthearted. "Is there another woman in the house?"

"No, actually, there isn't. I thought you knew, seeing as how you sponsored her. I mean, I assumed... We all assumed..."

Kenyon tried to make sense of that and failed. "Assumed that I knew what?"

"About Sabre, of course."

Kenyon sat up very straight. Something was wrong with his Sabre. Something had gone very wrong and he hadn't been there to help. He felt the beginnings of panic and gripped the receiver so hard it shook with his hand.

"What about Sabre? Where is she? What's happened?"

Garrick was infuriatingly slow to respond. "I'm sure it's all for the best," he observed idly. "Likely it would have turned out the same way in the end. However, I can't help being a little disappointed. A real Garrick just doesn't give up like that."

"Give up? Give up? What the hell are you talking about, man?"

"The inheritance, of course. I'm ready to have the papers drawn up."

Kenyon would've throttled him, if he could have reached through the phone to get him. As it was, he came to his feet.

"What about Sabre?" he demanded, his free hand going to his waist. He hadn't sacrificed all those weeks, put in all that hard work, ground his teeth and kept his hands to himself—mostly—for nothing. What happened to that woman was important to him, damned important, and he'd have told her so himself if she hadn't ... What? Fallen out of love with him? But that supposed she had been in love with him. *I wanted to make love with you, Kenyon. I think you're beautiful, too.* He sat down again, suddenly weak, and realized Garrick was talking.

"So, naturally, Darryl is the only choice. I trust you'll draw up the papers at once, or would you rather I contacted Pantier about this?"

Kenyon's mind was racing. Darryl was the heir, then. Sweet, sincere, loving Sabre was out. How unfair. How grossly, horribly unfair, and he suddenly didn't care who knew it.

"You stupid old goat!" he told him. "How could you do this to her? That woman wanted to love you. She's desperately poor, Garrick, but still your money was *not* as important to her as your love and respect. That was the goal. That's why she did her damnedest to be what you wanted. And she succeeded, too. Sabre can hold her own with anybody, anywhere, and even those snobs you hang around with know it!"

"I quite agree."

"You bet your boo— What?"

"I said, I quite agree. Sabre is a most remarkable young woman. She has a lot to learn yet, of course, but I've no doubt she'll do us proud in the end."

Kenyon was momentarily speechless. "Then why write her out?"

The answer was a shocker. "Because she asked me to."

"Asked you to?"

"Before she left, she stated in no uncertain terms that she wouldn't accept—I believe the phrase was 'a filthy penny' from me." Kenyon's eyes were wide as saucers. His heart was pounding like a sledgehammer.

"Left?" he repeated. "She left? Where? Where'd she go? She didn't go back to the bayou?" He had a sudden vision of that ape Goula, and Sabre's angry words came back to him. *At least with Ami Goula I know what to expect.*

Garrick was speaking again, saying he really didn't know where she'd gone. Kenyon didn't wait to hear more. "I have to go," he said, and hung up. Without missing a beat, he hit the intercom button. "Kathy, get me a seat on the next plane going to New Orleans, and I do mean the next." He got up and reached for his suit coat.

"Boss," his secretary's voice came back, "your mother's here, and she wants to see you."

He rolled his eyes, throwing on his coat. "I don't have time to see her now. I—I'll call her. Tell her—"

The door opened and Patsy Ames walked in. Sixty, fit, and remarkably attractive, she trailed fox tails and a Gucci scarf.

"Hello, sweetheart," she said, making a show of removing her gloves. "What's this about you running off to New Orleans, again?"

He tried not to seem impatient. "Mom, I love you. It's great to see you. I'll call you soon. Now, I'm sorry, but I've gotta go."

Patsy Ames put on her tolerant smile and calmly walked over and closed the door. "Now, Kenyon," she said, "it's not like you to keep so much to yourself. You're always talking about your work, always offering the most entertaining stories, but after more than three months of almost continual absence, I've yet to hear a single detail. That's not like you."

Kenyon sighed and pinched the bridge of his nose. "This is personal," he began. Patsy Ames smiled triumphantly.

"A woman. Well, well. Might I ask her name?"

Kenyon put both hands into his pants pockets, nervously jingling his change and car keys. "Sabre Callot. Now I really have to go."

"Callot?" Patsy mused. "I don't believe I recall the name."

Kenyon took a long breath. "You won't find it in the social register, if that's what you mean."

"No? Didn't come out, did she? I don't know why so many young women of status are so loath to be labeled debutantes. Both of your sisters-in-law made a proper debut. Oh, well, who is she?"

Kenyon looked his mother in the face, prepared to say that Sabre was the granddaughter of Vanguard Garrick of the New Orleans Garricks, very old money, very old society, very aristocratic, with roots his own second-generation family wealth couldn't possibly match. She would be a proper catch, provided no one mentioned the nearly illiterate, half-drunk father from the bayou, the lack of "proper schooling," the Cajun accent. He could have painted a picture rosy enough to keep his mother satisfied for some time to come, but at the last minute, he just knew he couldn't. His face turned red from the embarrassment of ever having started to justify the existence of a woman named Sabre Callot and his feelings for her. He struck a relaxed pose and folded his arms, smiling the first truly guiltless smile he'd smiled since he'd first laid eyes on the bayou woman.

"Sabre Callot," he said, "is a sweet, simple, unaffected nobody." His mother recoiled a bit, surprised. "Did I say beautiful? I should have said beautiful. And smart and unselfish and loving and passionate. In short, Mother, Sabre Callot is no one, except the woman I love."

Patsy Ames stared at her son, apparently weighing his sincerity. Then she shrugged and folded her manicured hands.

"When do I get to meet her?"

Kenyon scratched his ear. "I'll let you know." He walked forward and opened the door of his office. Patsy Ames laid a restraining hand on his shoulder. He sent her a sharp, level glare. She smiled apologetically and hugged him. "Goodbye," he said. "Wish me luck."

"I do," she assured him, but he was already gone.

Finding people was what he did best, after all. He started with the three Garricks themselves, but learned only that Sabre had announced about ten days earlier that she had a job and was moving out on her own. There had been a row. Van had accused her of being ungrateful and foolish, but he secretly admitted to Kenyon that he admired her determination and pride. He wished her well, but couldn't say where she'd gone or for whom she was working. Neither Darryl nor Mallory offered anything but acrimony. Kenyon guessed at each sensed Van's growing regard for their kins-woman, but it didn't really matter. All that mattered was finding her.

Theo told him she'd talked about saving money for college, which made a lot of sense, and that she had promised to get in touch as soon as things were settled. But he conceded that she had not known where she was going when he had left. All he knew for sure was that she had intended to locate near "the university." But which university would that be? Besides Loyola and Tulane, there were several more: Newcomb, Dillard, Delgado J.C., the University of New Orleans, and others.

Kenyon was so relieved to hear that she hadn't left immediately for the bayou and Ami Goula that he didn't care how many areas he had to check out, but he did feel a certain pressure. While he was focusing on this, his practice was at a standstill. And there was always the chance that Sabre would find someone else, or that someone else would find her, and he knew now he couldn't let that happen. He hired help and outlined the procedure. It was early yet, but a person had to leave some kind of a trail. They started checking out registrars' offices and the utility companies. Hospitals were a real long shot, but they made the calls, anyway.

What worried Kenyon most was that she couldn't have had much money. It was Theo's guess that she'd been actually working for a week or more before she'd packed up some boxes and moved out. She'd been stepping out a lot at different times of the day and evening without saying where she was going. Kenyon wondered what kind of job that could be and how much money she could have scraped together during that time. Fortunately, Theo had an idea about that.

It seemed that a day or so after the dinner party, he and Sabre had taken a stroll around Jackson Square and had stopped to watch a particular painter at work. The artist had

noticed and paused to strike up a conversation. He had told
Sabre that she would make an exceptional model, and Sabre
had asked how much she could earn. Theo hadn't thought
much about it at the time, but now he couldn't help wondering if she'd been thinking of leaving even then.

Kenyon went to Jackson Square every day for five days,
and on the fifth he saw a painting of Sabre propped against
a wrought-iron fence. She was wearing an antebellum gown
à la Scarlett O'Hara and sitting in a window seat staring
dreamily into space, her reflection staring back from
darkened window glass. He bought the painting and grilled
the artist.

Yes, Sabre had modeled for him, and he'd paid her
handsomely. He had suggested she apply at one of the
universities for a full-time job as an artist's model, but she'd
been disenchanted when told the position would probably
require her to pose in the nude. She'd remarked that she'd
rather wait tables, scrub floors, baby-sit. It was back to
square one. Then one evening, he was buying a soft drink
in a convenience store and happened to glance at a rack of
paperback novels. That was when it hit him.

Forty-eight hours later, he'd arranged stakeouts at every
library branch in the greater New Orleans area. It was cost-
ing him a fortune—but it paid off.

Kenyon sat on the McIlhaneys' couch and smiled apologetically. He felt like an interloper in this stylishly middle-
class suburban home. He covered his wristwatch with his
hand in an effort not to look at it just one more time, and
cleared his throat. Mr. McIlhaney started in his chair as
he'd almost dropped off to sleep. Mrs. McIlhaney, perched
beside him, laid a hand on his arm and returned Kenyon's
apologetic smile.

"I can't imagine what's keeping her," she said, for perhaps the fifth time. "Are you sure she was expecting you, Mr. Ames?"

Kenyon crossed his legs and lied smoothly. "Quite sure."

Mr. McIlhaney stifled a yawn and sniffed loudly to clear his sinuses. "She's teaching our three-year-old French," he said. "Did we tell you she was teaching our three-year-old French?"

Kenyon nodded. "Yes, I believe you did."

"He's our little scholar," Mrs. McIlhaney said of her son, who was sleeping peacefully in another room. "We're so lucky to have found Sabre. She's great with the kids. The baby loves her."

"Um, it's a good situation," put in Mr. McIlhaney, stifling another yawn. "She's here all day with the children, but she leaves as soon as my wife gets home. This second job of hers sometimes keeps her out until one or two in the morning, though. Good thing she's young. Can't get much sleep. I just wish she could drive a car. We have to depend on the neighbors to get our son to and from music lessons. We use the Suzuki method. Did we tell you we use the Suzuki method?"

Kenyon nodded. "Yes, I believe you did."

A long silence followed, after which Mrs. McIlhaney said, "I can't imagine what's keeping her. Are you sure she was expecting you?"

Kenyon ground his teeth then reinforced his smile. "What time did you say she was supposed to get in tonight?"

Fortunately, the McIlhaneys did not have to answer that question as from the back of the house came the cracking sound of a weather-stripped door opening. Mrs. McIlhaney brightened, and ten or fifteen seconds later, Sabre walked into the living room, wearing the crisp gray-and-white uniform of a waitress, complete with cap. Kenyon came instantly to his feet, his heart lurching at the sight of her.

"Kenyon!"

That was as much recognition as the McIlhaneys needed to be satisfied that they hadn't allowed an impostor into their neat, little used living room. Mr. McIlhaney hauled himself up, stretched and yawned unreservedly.

"We'll leave you two alone. Nice to meet you, Mr. Ames. Doris, let's go to bed."

Kenyon barely heard them. He was looking at the expression on Sabre's face, trying to decide if she was glad to see him or not. As the McIlhaneys left the room, she reached up and unpinned the starched cap. Her dark auburn hair was held in a long, thick ponytail placed high on the back of her head.

"How did you find me?" she asked in a low voice. Kenyon shrugged. Even nervous and uncertain of his welcome, he couldn't help smiling.

"Finding people is a big part of what I do for a living," he said.

She nodded her understanding and sighed. "I guess I just didn't think you'd come looking for me again."

"I didn't think you'd just disappear without letting me know where you were going."

She passed a hand over her face. "Look, Kenyon, if this is about the money I owe you, I want you to know I intend to pay back every cent."

"What money? This isn't about money." He shook his head. "I don't care about money."

She held the cap in both hands, studying it. He noticed she was biting her lip, and that made him grin. It was one of those naturally, unconsciously pouty things she did, so unaffected it was truly charming. *Eat your heart out, Karen,* he thought.

"Isn't it strange," she said, "how only those people with money can afford not to care about it?"

He supposed it was true, and he realized anew that there was, indeed, this gulf between them, but he'd been thinking about closing it, and he thought he knew how he could do that—if he could convince her to go along.

"You know, Sabre, it wasn't very kind of you to go off without letting all the people who care about you know where to find you."

"And who would that be?" she retorted with surprising venom.

He had to think about how it must have seemed to her all the while she'd been trying so hard to be what all those aloof, unloving people wanted her to be. He had been part of that, he knew, but no more. He moved closer, fighting the impulse to take her in his arms. He didn't dare, not after what had happened the last time. *Coward,* he chided himself. *She's been dealing with rejection all this time, and you can't bring yourself to risk it even now.*

"You'd be surprised to know who really cares," he told her quietly. "But, ah, what about your father and brother?"

She shifted her eyes away guiltily. "I didn't want them to worry about me being out on my own. I'll contact them as soon as I . . . Soon."

"You were going to say as soon as you had enough money, weren't you?" She didn't reply, just cast about the room for something upon which to fix her gaze. He took another step forward, searching for the arguments he needed. "Don't you see? It's too much for one person to do alone. You can't do everything you're trying to do, at one time. You can't save enough money to bring them here and go to college and send Butler to college and pay me back what you think you owe me. You just can't do it all at once!"

She looked away, and he realized suddenly that she wa
fighting tears. He felt awful, just awful.

"I'm sorry," he whispered, but she turned her back
struggling for composure. He winced. "That's right. I'
forgotten. I robbed that expression of a good deal of it
meaning. Overuse, I think. But then I've had a lot to b
sorry about."

She shook her head, sniffing. "No, that's all right. I'
just tired." She turned back to him, chewing her lip. "I—
didn't think it would be so hard, any of it." She lifted a hand
to her forehead and stepped away from him, wandering ove
to the chair where Mr. McIlhaney had nodded off. She sa
down and fingered the cap in her lap nervously. "The trut
is, I wouldn't have made it this far, if it hadn't been for you
I was so naive. I knew it would be difficult, but I thought i
I tried hard enough I could win Grandfather over."

"I think you've accomplished more on that front tha
you think you have," he told her confidently. "He told m
how much he respects your decision to go out on your own
however ill-advised."

She cast him a hopeful look, but immediately aban
doned it. "I'm sure Mallory doesn't share his opinion."

"I'm sure she doesn't. Darryl, either. But that's thei
problem."

"He won't go against her," she said, but he shrugged.

"I don't know. He might. Eventually. In fact, I think h
will."

She stared up at him, and for the first time he could se
that she was really trying to divine his reason for being here
He couldn't tell what she was thinking, hoping. He wen
down on his haunches in front of her, one hand going to he
knee, the other to her chin. She wasn't wearing stockings
he noticed, and that made him want to laugh. She wasn't so
terribly different then, his Sabre, his wonderful, simpl
Sabre. But her chin was a little wobbly, and she tugged self

consciously at the hem of her skirt. He removed his hands, wondering if that was distaste at his touch or something more promising. There was one sure way to find out. He steeled himself.

"Look, I know I don't have any right to ask, but...could you come with me for a while? It's important, Sabre. I wouldn't ask, otherwise."

Maybe it was the look on his face or the tone of his voice or something for which he dared not hope. Whatever the reason, she stared at him a long, loaded moment, then quickly nodded.

"All right, Kenyon. It's the least I can do. Give me a moment to change."

He felt suddenly weak and then frightened. *Step one,* he told himself. *A beginning but just that.* He got up and moved back, giving her room to leave the chair. She slipped out, and he heard the low murmur of voices from another part of the house. He supposed she was telling the McIlhaneys she was going out again. He wondered what they thought, if she would insist on staying with them, who they would get to care for their children if she left them. So many loose ends. He paced the room, the tension building in him with every step, but then she was back, her hair falling luxuriously about her shoulders. She was wearing jeans and a big pink sweater with a soft collar and a three-button placket. On her feet were high-topped pink tennis shoes.

"Is this all right?" she asked, and he squelched the desire to laugh happily.

"It's great! But I didn't buy you those things."

She lifted her chin in that determined way of hers, and he wanted to reach out and bring her to him and just hold her there.

"Well, maybe it wasn't the thing to do, but I just wanted to buy something for myself. They weren't expensive. You know, you can find pretty nice stuff at the discount stores."

He disciplined a wiggly grin. "I think it's great," he said. "And I'll bet those things feel better than anything I bought you."

She looked sheepish, uncomfortable. "I wouldn't go that far." She hesitated a moment, then gave in to impulse, rolling her eyes. "I can't stand cheap stockings!" she admitted explosively, and he did laugh, gently, circumspectly. She pushed her hair back, glaring, then softened and laughed with him.

"Come on, *chérie*," he said, imitating her accent. "The night isn't getting any younger."

He escorted her outside and put her in the car he had rented, then got behind the wheel. Midcity was not so far away from where they had to go. He drove down to Carrollton, then went up to Canal and headed toward the river. Within minutes they were turning into the French Quarter, making their way through narrow streets crowded with parked vehicles and the occasional taxi. They even passed a one-horse dray, the driver allowing his charge to plod along while the couple in the back occupied themselves in a rather passionate clinch.

"We're not going to Grandfather's?" she asked when they turned off into the Vieux Carré.

"No," he said, shooting her a loaded glance. "We're going back to the place where we jumped off track."

"What?" She was looking at him with the most perplexed expression, but he resisted the temptation to just burst out with it.

"You'll see," he said, hoping she actually would.

He parked the car about a block away rather than risk driving by the place and tipping his hand too early. She didn't say anything when they got out, but she did take a long look around. He took her by the arm and propelled her along the sidewalk, hurrying not only out of nervousness but from a need to recreate the moment as completely as he could. She didn't say anything until they were almost there, and then she didn't say what he expected her to.

"Has your friend come back from...wherever?" She waved a hand. His pulse was beating in his temples like a pair of kettle drums, and his mouth was as dry as cotton. He already had the keys out of his pocket and in his hand.

"No," he said shortly, tossing the key. "Look, um, you may not want to come up, but I—I have to." He turned abruptly and strode away, fighting the impulse to see if she would follow. His hand was shaking as he fitted the key into the gate's metal lock. Some demon seemed to be spurring him on, telling him to move faster and faster. He yanked open the gate and bounded up the stairs, taking them two at a time. Then he moved along the landing and—the key went in smoothly, thank God—into the apartment. He left the door open and stepped quickly into the hall, putting his back to the wall, calming himself with deep, measured breathing. It was only a moment, but it seemed an hour before he heard her on the landing.

He closed his eyes and let his breath out slowly. The door closed, and she called his name. He stepped into the open doorway, real hope taking hold now.

"Well, come on," he said. "This way." She just looked at him, and then she started across the floor. He turned and walked into the bedroom, checking to be certain all was in order. He'd opened the curtains so that light spilled in through the window from the courtyard. It was sufficient. Clothing was scattered around the room, some of it neatly arranged, some of it haphazard. He turned to meet her as she entered the room, and his hand flew up to his head. He pushed his fingers through his hair and swallowed hard.

"It's not afternoon, obviously, but...I didn't want to wait any longer. I couldn't wait for another time."

She licked her lips and glanced round the room, taking it all in, and brought her gaze back to him. "What are you going to do?'' she asked, her voice was small and trembling. He took a step forward and reached for her hand, his free arm going about her waist.

''What I should have done the first time,'' he told her softly, stepping off to the waltz playing in his head. She followed easily, her eyes large and wary and shining. He led her gently to the white shirt and stopped. She looked down at it, and then she carefully moved her foot and lifted her toe, as if to step on it. That was when he knew for sure that she understood.

''I love you,'' he said, ''and I want to make love with you.''

She gazed up at him, her mouth slightly open, her chest heaving with labored breath. Then she very carefully knelt on the floor. He went down on his knees and took her in his arms, his mouth brushing hers. For a long time he simply held her and tried to find his voice, but in the end it was she who spoke.

''I love you, too,'' she whispered, ''and I want to make love with you, but—''

''No buts,'' he said, pulling her face back to gaze into those golden eyes.

''Will you marry me, then?'' she asked timidly, and he began to laugh. He sat on the floor, one knee drawn up.

''I think we'd better get some things settled right now,'' he said. ''I want to live right here in the French Quarter. We'll get a place big enough for Butler and your father, and we'll worry about room enough for kids later. Now, then, about the wedding—''

She launched herself at him, howling with glee, and he let her bowl him over onto his back. It was just a matter of rolling over, then, to have her right where he wanted her, there at the very place where he'd blown it before. But that wasn't going to happen again. Somehow, while she was busy becoming the Sabre she had always been waiting to be, he had become the Kenyon he should have been, and they were a perfect match. Not that there wasn't a lot left to do. She would have questions, and he couldn't blame her. He'd been an awful fool, and he'd known it even before that day in the park. She'd never know how close she'd come to breaking his heart that day. And there were other things, happy things.

She wanted to go to college, and she was going to get that chance. She deserved a grandfather who took pride in her, and he wasn't going to rest until that happened for her. His father-in-law—*future* father-in-law—was going to need some medical care, and Butler... He could just see them all together, sitting around the table in the parlor talking over some obscure book or a recent case. He was going to have to bring in a young partner, someone who could do the leg-work and endure long absences. He wasn't going anywhere for a long, long time. Life was going to be exciting enough for him right here at home. Quite exciting enough.

*   *   *   *   *

Silhouette ❦ *Romance*

COMING NEXT MONTH

#706 NEVER ON SUNDAE—Rita Rainville
A Diamond Jubilee Title!
Heather Brandon wanted to help women lose weight. But lean, hard Wade Mackenzie had different ideas. He wanted Heather to lose her heart—to him!

#707 DOMESTIC BLISS—Karen Leabo
By working as a maid, champion of women's rights Spencer Guthrie tried to prove he practiced what he preached. But could he convince tradition-minded Bonnie Chapman that he loved a woman like her?

#708 THE MARK OF ZORRO—Samantha Grey
Once conservative Sarah Wingate saw "the man in the mask" she couldn't keep her thoughts on co-worker Jeff Baxter. But then she learned he and Zorro were one and the same!

#709 A CHILD CALLED MATTHEW—Sara Grant
Laura Bryant was determined to find her long-lost son at any cost. Then she discovered the key to the mystery lay with Gareth Ryder, the man who had once broken her heart.

#710 TIGER BY THE TAIL—Pat Tracy
Sarah Burke had grown up among tyrants, so Lucas Rockworth's gentle demeanor drew her like a magnet. Soon, however, she learned her lamb roared like a lion!

#711 SEALED WITH A KISS—Joan Smith
Impetuous Jodie James was off with stuffy—but handsome!—Greg Edison to look for their missing brothers. Jodie knew they were a mismatched couple, but she was starting to believe the old adage that opposites attract....

AVAILABLE THIS MONTH:

You'll flip . . . your pages won't!
Read paperbacks *hands-free* with

Book Mate · I

The perfect "mate" for all your romance paperbacks

Traveling • Vacationing • At Work • In Bed • Studying • Cooking • Eating

Perfect size for all standard paperbacks, this wonderful invention makes reading a pure pleasure! Ingenious design holds paperback books OPEN and FLAT so even wind can't ruffle pages— leaves your hands free to do other things. Reinforced, wipe-clean vinyl- covered holder flexes to let you turn pages without undoing the strap . . . supports paperbacks so well, they have the strength of hardcovers!

Pages turn WITHOUT opening the strap

SEE-THROUGH STRAP

Reinforced back stays flat

Built in bookmark

BOOK MARK

BACK COVER HOLDING STRIP

10" x 7¼" opened
Snaps closed for easy carrying, too

Available now. Send your name, address, and zip code, along with a check or money order for just $5.95 + .75¢ for postage & handling (for a total of $6.70) payable to Reader Service to:

Reader Service
Bookmate Offer
901 Fuhrmann Blvd.
P.O. Box 1396
Buffalo, N.Y. 14269-1396

Offer not available in Canada
*New York and Iowa residents add appropriate sales tax.

BM-G

At long last, the books you've been waiting for
by one of America's top romance authors!

DIANA PALMER

DUETS

Ten years ago Diana Palmer published her very first
romances. Powerful and dramatic, these gripping tales
of love are everything you have come to expect from
Diana Palmer.

In March, some of these titles will be available again in
DIANA PALMER DUETS—a special three-book collection. Each book will have two wonderful stories plus an
introduction by the author. You won't want to miss them!

Book 1
SWEET ENEMY
LOVE ON TRIAL

Book 2
STORM OVER THE LAKE
TO LOVE AND CHERISH

Book 3
IF WINTER COMES
NOW AND FOREVER

 *Silhouette Books*®

DP-1